MALLARDS REVISITED

More sacred & profane memories of
Mapp & Lucia in E.F.Benson's Tilling

Deryck J. Solomon

Haseley Grange Publishing

With love to John, David and Winnie, my family

CONTENTS

INTRODUCTION

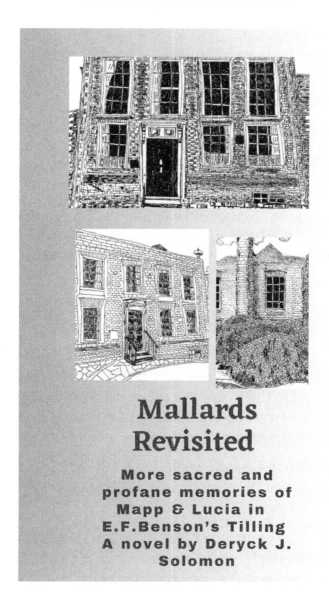

Mallards Revisited

More sacred and profane memories of Mapp & Lucia in E.F.Benson's Tilling A novel by Deryck J. Solomon

I enjoyed revisiting my vision of the world of Emmeline Pillson, otherwise known as "Lucia," and Elizabeth Mapp-Flint in Tilling created by E.F.Benson in my trilogy of novels centred upon its senior police officer.

Beginning with "Inspector Morrison's Case Book," his career continued with "Inspector Morrison: Another Year in Tilling" and drew to a close with "Inspector Morrison's Casebook Concluded."

Herbert Morrison's story began with a prequel covering his childhood in Tilling and introducing us to friends such as Georgie and Per and prominent figures such as the the spinster owner of Mallards, Caroline Mapp and her youthful niece Elizabeth.

In that early account, we learn how Elizabeth Mapp came to be left Mallards and the final part of this book explores the longer term consequences of how this inheritance was secured so many years before.

The departure of Inspector Morrison from Tilling gave an opportunity to focus again upon many old friends.

We are able to revisit familiar themes such as Major Benjy's drinking habits, the iconoclasm of Quaint Irene Coles and her controversial work, the many Macchiavellian traits of Elizabeth Mapp-Flint and even the perpetually questionable character of Diva Plaistow's infamous sardine tartlets.

As must always be the case on any visit to Tilling, the personality and sheer life force of the chatelaine of Mallards and Mayor, Lucia permeates the red-roofed town on its ancient hill.

As ever, she is loyally supported by her eternal cavalier serviente, Georgie Pillson through new trials and tribulations often caused or at least exacerbated by her perpetual rival and Mayoress,

Elizabeth Mapp-Flint.

If there is a theme to these stories, it is the impulse to return or revisit, its desirability and consequences and the possibility of redemption.

My consistent objective in returning to E.F.Benson's Tilling is to respect the spirit of his magical creation and to try to leave it as I found it.

I confess to departing from this rule in reporting the tragic choux-related passing of celebrated novelist Susan Leg, who was believed to be based on E.F.Benson's nemesis, Marie Corelli. For this I crave your indulgence and hope that otherwise I have honoured "our Fred."

I do hope you enjoy your visit.

Until next time, Au reservoir

Deryck Solomon
Haseley,
July 2023

CHAPTER ONE: AU RESERVOIR INSPECTOR MORRISON

On the turn of the year, Tilling learned of the elevation of its distinguished Mayor and Senior Police Officer to the rank of Dame and Knight of the Order of the British Empire.

Both honourees had dutifully stood before their new monarch at Buckingham Palace and humbly accepted the award universally recognised as "as richly deserved, as it was unexpected."

After the investiture in the gilt splendour of the Ballroom, the historic event was recorded by cheerful press photographs on the gravelled forecourt which soon made their way to the front page of the "Tilling Gazette."

Inside, a full page spread set out candid shots under a headline proclaiming "Tilling's most glorious day."

There followed exclusive interviews graciously granted by the Mayor and "her Inspector" to the Gazette's veteran senior reporter Oswald Meriton.

Always the most devoted admirer of she whom he dubbed "the chatelaine of Mallards House," Mr Meriton's breathless encomium groaned under a superfluity of sugary adjectives, positively life-threatening to any diabetic reader.

Predictably, leading figures in the town viewed the great honour bestowed upon their community in a traditionally aloof manner.

Their approach equated to Tilling's own version of the psychological stages of grief following bereavement. Initial resentful scepticism, irritation and distaste was soon substituted with a steadfast denial that any such event had ever taken place. It was simply never mentioned.

After years of relentlessly scaling all possible social and civic peaks in the locality, Emmeline Pillson had gained a thorough understanding of the inclination of her closest intimes to resent her success. Others might consider that their approach stemmed from a positively teutonic Schadenfreude.

Dame Emmeline addressed the wilful refusal to acknowledge her deserved elevation and that of "her" Inspector by entertaining her closest friends who constituted the cream of Tilling society at considerable expense at a stylish Devon hotel for the weekend.

There, at the streamlined, white temple to the moderne on Burgh Island close to Bigbury on Sea, the guests accepting the Mayor's celebratory hospitality were forced to acknowledge the great honour bestowed upon their community by His Majesty, albeit through gritted teeth otherwise happily appeased in dispatching considerable quantities the finest Devon crustacea and sublime

French vintages.

It was understood that immediately after the Investiture the new young Queen Elizabeth had expressed her personal pleasure upon this occasion and admitted to being "simply thrilled," thus forever relegating the confirmation of the former Queen Mary that Her Majesty was "so pleased" about the award of the MBE to Susan Wyse some years before to obscurity.

In typical fashion, great pleasure was felt in dear Susan's effective demotion and the term "every cloud" was heard more than once.

Now that her circle had acknowledged her new status and publicly demonstrated their fealty ("bowed for their supper," so to speak), the Dame (as some still sarcastically had come to refer to her whilst her back was turned) felt secure enough to beseech her dear friends to continue as before "as though the great honour bestowed upon me by His Majesty had never taken place."

Wishing to be seen to be merciful, as was her practice, Lucia continued, "Of course, in private, my title never need be heard, although I appreciate that, contrary to my own personal wishes, and as an addition to my many burdens as a public servant, I will be obliged to hear my formal title employed on civic or magisterial occasions, since any other mode of address might be deemed to demonstrate a lack of respect towards His Majesty, by whom it was so generously conferred. In Tilling that would never do."

To mark the end of their effective and, at times, dramatic working relationship as senior Police Officer and Civic Head of Tilling, Lucia was pleased to host a dinner at Mallards at which the great and good of the town and county might express their thinks for his valued contribution.

That evening as the clock on the Norman tower of St Mary's Church struck seven, lights shone through the Georgian casement windows to the street below as guests arrived at the varnished black door which so resembled that in Downing Street some miles due north.

As the company gathered in the drawing room, maids Foljambe and Grosvenor offered silver trays bearing champagne and cook's finest canapes.

Whilst Georgie Pillson chatted to Bunty Morrison, Lucia circulated introducing the guest of honour to her guests beginning with Lord Ardingly, the Lord Lieutenant of the County with Lady Ardingly.

Herbert had known everyone present for many years at the helm of Tilling's police and no introductions were really necessary; the prevailing atmosphere was convivial and relaxed.

In one corner of the drawing room prominent residents the Mapp-Flints chatted animatedly with the Wyses.

Absorbed in conversation with Susan Wyse, Elizabeth Mapp failed to prevent her husband Major Benjy from securing a third flute of champagne in the remarkably short interval since his arrival.

Given that the purpose of the gathering was to celebrate the career of Tilling's senior police officer, it was hardly surprising that pre-dinner conversation was centred upon the many dramatic highlights of Inspector Morrison's career.

Elizabeth Mapp-Flint recalled the dark afternoon when Major Benjy's embittered housekeeper had tried to murder her with a poisoned sardine tartlet at Ye Olde Tea Shoppe. Since that day neither Elizabeth nor her husband had given a single thought to his loyal but deranged servant who still languished forgotten and unvisited in a prison cell in Maidstone in the next county

The memory only prompted Elizabeth to complain pointedly to Diva Plaistow, "Since that day I have never been able to force down one of those questionable fishy savouries,"

"Your loss entirely Elizabeth," retorted Diva, "One of my most popular lines. Everyone else, enjoys them enormously."

"Now, dear ladies," intervened Algernon Wyse, "Water under the bridge. Let us remember why we are here this evening. We all recognise that the insight and deductive power of our Inspector solved the mystery with remarkable speed."

"Absolutely Algernon dear," added Susan breathlessly seeking to fill the glaring silence left by Elizabeth and Diva, "We will be eternally grateful for the Inspector's brilliance in exposing that ghastly fraudulent medium who tormented me so cruelly and exploited my love of my dear, departed Blue Birdie."

"And catching the tragic murderer of poor Dolly Brace," observed Diva.

"Not forgetting apprehending the one responsible for stealing our Christmas Club Savings," added Elizabeth, not wanting to be outdone, "He certainly saved our Christmas that year."

"How true, Elizabeth," said Diva, signifying a truce after their earlier tartlet-induced spat.

"Of course, Inspector Morrison was very understanding to my Benjy during his difficult times," continued Elizabeth recognising that the best way to minimise possibly embarrassing recollections was to address the issue and swiftly move on.

Fully recognising this, the group skirted around the Major's several disappearances and scandalous revelations concerning the mythical Pride of Poona and of both a long-lost son and granddaughter. All that needed to be understood on what was to be Inspector Morrison's evening was his huge part in peacefully resolving a series of serious crimes and personal crises.

In another corner of the drawing room, the Padre and Evie Bartlett shared memories with Quaint Irene Coles, whose severe evening suit and manly haircut gave her a startling resemblance to controversial author Radclyffe Hall.

"Of course, Inspector Morrison saved our bacon when dear Lucy and I were kidnapped by those bandits in Sicily," explained Irene.

"How can we ever forget? You must have been terrified!" exclaimed Evie, whose pitch increased with every syllable, "We were all so concerned, we hardly slept."

"You needn't have worried," remarked Irene casually, "My dear Lucia made sure her Inspector sorted everything out and we were then quite safe. In fact, Turrido was quite a sweetie."

"For a ruthless Sicilian bandit," added the Padre drily.

"No, really," explained Irene, "The locals worshipped him and looked on him as a kind of Robin Hood, robbing the rich to give to the poor. And he loved his family. He couldn't do enough for us, especially after the Inspector talked him round and I offered to paint his mother's portrait. In fact, we still exchange Christmas cards. However, it was Inspector Morrison who understood all that sonic business and uncovered his better side. Herbert saved us and I shall always be grateful to him."

"To be sure, to be sure," confirmed the Padre, slipping into Irish brogue for the first time that evening.

Since his eventful visit to Burgh Island and enforced confrontation with his chequered past within Birmingham's criminal underworld, the Reverend Bartlett had quite returned to his old self with his many and varied vocal quirks and mannerisms.

The Padre's repertoire of dialects and brogues of the United Kingdom continued to be exploited as relentlessly as before, but had been expanded by the addition of the odd phrase from the argot or patois of the nation's second city and the Black Country to the north.

The Padre's already richly diverse speech patterns were expanded even further by the addition of the occasional interrogative "Oirright?" sometimes with the additional informal diminutive "bab" appended.

The first occasion the Padre greeted Lady Ardingly, "Oirright bab?" before Sunday service caused a sensation amongst church-going circles in Tilling and indeed throughout the county.

Generally, however, the Padre's parishioners and friends were pleased that their pastor had been relieved of a lifetime of doubt over his questionable origins and freed from what had been a heavy burden of anxiety.

The Padre continued, "As ye know Miss Coles, ma wee wifie Evie and I also have good reason to be grateful to the guid Inspector and will never forget his kindness."

Before long, although not before Major Benjy had dispatched his sixth glass of champagne, the company was called into dinner.

Hostess Lucia led the way to the dining room with guest of honour her Inspector, followed by Georgie Pillson escorting Bunty Morrison and Lord and Lady Ardingly.

The other guests followed in an orderly but animated un-titled crocodile and dinner was served.

As the upper echelons in Tilling had come to expect, no expense or trouble was spared in the dinner that evening.

Thoughtful touches included service of Elizabeth Mapp's favourite pate de foie gras and everyone's perfect entree in Lucia's legendary Lobster a la Riseholme.

Experience had taught Foljambe and Grosvenor serving at table to try to moderate Major Benjy's intake of alcohol.

Despite their best efforts, however, his relentlessly swift

consumption and brazen and unstoppable demands for replenishment meant that he succeeded in imbibing prodigious quantities of the fine wine on offer.

The Major's remorseless Bacchic quest was punctuated with appreciative outbursts of praise addressed to no-one in particular and the world in general endorsing "such stunning foie gras," "that legendary lobster" and "historic Montrachet, what?"

Elizabeth Mapp's eyes narrowed as she viewed her life partner's enthusiastic appreciation of his "damn fine dinner" increase in duration and volume as the evening progressed. Unfortunately his palpable treachery was often compounded by loud dismissive comparisons with the "meagre rations on offer out at Grebe."

Not unused to this turn of events, Elizabeth somehow succeeded in masking her increasing fury and frustration. Her demeanour did not hint at the anger within, save for the regular throbbing of a small vein in her right temple, discernible to only the most experienced and observant of her intimes.

What everyone at table that evening knew was that the only certainty in life that night was that in the morning Major Benjy would pay for his transgressions many times over.

As had been proven over the years, his good lady wife's revenge would be both as prompt and terrible as it was inevitable.

Filet mignon was succeeded by Lucia's speciality dessert of raspberry souffle. All agreed that dinner had been sublime and that Lucia's dedicated cook had excelled her already spectacular reputation.

Tactfully, out of consideration to Susan Wyse, no-one mentioned the unfortunate immolation of the stuffed cadaver of Blue Birdie within the same delicious dessert at this very dining table some years before.

Whilst the last plate was cleared, the Mayor rose from her place at the head of the table.

The guests anticipated a florid speech of praise and thanks to the Senior Officer of the town's constabulary by their hostess as Mayor and Chief Magistrate followed by a paean in similar vein by Lord Ardingly as Lord Lieutenant of the County and the direct representative of His Majesty in the locality.

After the presentation of a suitable expression of the appreciation of the citizens of Tilling for his invaluable contribution to the security and well being of their community over the years, such as a clock or engraved salver, Inspector Morrison would, no doubt, respond with thanks for the honour done to him and Lady Bunty on this glittering occasion and humble thanks for the touching keepsake which he would treasure forever as a physical embodiment of his many happy years fighting crime in the town.

Instead of launching into the anticipated peroration, Lucia surprised her guess by stating simply, "Lord and Lady Ardingly, Sir Herbert and Lady Bunty, Ladies and Gentlemen, I trust you enjoyed your dinner. Now to bring our evening to a close, please might I ask you to adjourn to the Garden Room where further refreshments will be served."

"I'll second that Your Worship' exclaimed Major Benjy, who having particularly enjoyed the exquisite wines served at dinner, now longed for a post-prandial digestif or several.

"Oh please do be quiet, Benjy," scowled Elizabeth Mapp, "You've had quite enough already. The last thing we need now is yet another po di mu by candlelight while Worship treats us to an agonisingly slow rendition of the easy part of that bit of beginner's Beethoven."

"I say Elizabeth old thing, that's a bit harsh, even for you. I quite like the Moonlight Serenade with a nice drop of brandy. 'S very relaxing, don't you think?" adding, to no-one in particular, "I'm devoted to Chopin, I am."

"Touched though I am by your enthusiasm for my playing, Major, I'm afraid I shall have to disappoint you and my dear Mayoress this evening," intervened Lucia in her most irritatingly soothing manner, "There will be no music tonight. I simply wished to invite my guests to move to the Garden Room to be more comfortable whilst we express a few words of thanks and make a presentation to mark our appreciation to our guest of honour on his last evening in Tilling."

"How very exciting and typically apt, Your Worship" chimed Algeron Wyse, shepherding the company from table towards the Garden Room, "What a fitting climax to a memorable evening. Pray lead the way, dearest hostess."

As the guests filed out to the dining room, Elizabeth and Benjamin Mapp-Flint brought up the rear somewhat sheepishly.

Inevitably, Elizabeth hissed the first salvo of a barrage of sour recriminations and warnings regarding the past and future conduct of her bibulous spouse into his unhearing ear.

By now however, the Major's sole preoccupation was anticipation of several glasses of fine brandy before the beginning of indefinite period of pain to be inflicted by his other half until the distant day of absolution came, if it ever did.

As more champagne and spirits were served, guests noted a large object some ten feet by six feet in size shrouded in a beribboned sheet with a gold-fringed tassel on an easel next to the grand piano in the window overlooking the cobbles that led to the High Street.

"Whatever now?" snapped Elizabeth irritably, waving away a tray of liqueurs tentatively proffered by Foljambe,

Soon, all was clear as their hostess again stood before them and began an authoritative review of her Inspector's career touching upon, "the celebrated cases solved by him and his massive contribution to the safety and well-being this fellow citizens. Born and bred in Tilling, Sir Herbert had become a hero of the town and had earned its eternal gratitude."

Lucia stressed the personal qualities of common sense and humility that contributed so much to his success and earned the respect of all. His self-effacement made it challenging to mark his achievements in a manner that he would find acceptable. "It has fallen to me to devise a fit and proper tribute to mark the career of a proud son of Tilling and, though I say it myself, I am confident that I have found a perfect solution to this conundrum."

"How unlike her to claim that she was the only one amongst us clever enough to work it out," muttered Elizabeth at a volume audible to everyone. A dark foreboding that what lurked beneath the sheet would be mortifying was rapidly engulfing her.

As Elizabeth literally gritted her formidable molars, Lucia called upon Lady Ardingly to do them all the honour of unveiling what rested upon the easel.

As Lady Ardingly performed the task not unfamiliar to her as consort of the Lord Lieutenant, there was audible communal intake of breath followed by several seconds of silence.

As the drapery cascaded to the carpeted floor of the Garden Room a striking tableau in oils came under scrutiny.

To universal surprise, the Mrs. Pillson's personal gift and tribute to her Inspector was seen to be composed of a virtually life-sized depiction of the Mayor of Tilling in full civic dress including a dashing feathered tricorn hat, ermine trimmed robe and gold chain of office astride what could best be described as the "official Mayoral tandem."

Smiling triumphantly at the front of the vehicle, the Mayor steered nonchalantly with one gloved hand whilst the other waved at the crowd of onlookers.

Looking closely, Georgie Pillson was pleased to be able to make out his own embroidery on the mayoral gauntlet. "Such neat work," he thought.

Behind the Mayor, managing to smile broadly whilst peddling assiduously, sat Inspector Morrison in full dress uniform with the prominent addition of the insignia of his recent honour.

As if the scene were not sufficiently triumphant, the artist had seen fit to set out in the extensive margins of the piece an exultant throng of cheering admirers, each casting bright nosegays, rose petals, cherry blossoms and even palm fronds beneath the tandem wheels. The portrait managed to combine both heroic and biblical cadences.

Closer inspection showed clearly that many members of the exultant crowd bore a starting resemblance to current leading citizens of the town.

Muttering ensued when the Padre discerned himself in clerical garb in an apparent act of benediction involving the dispensation of liberal quantities of Holy Water.

Algernon and Susan Wyse felt sure it was they who were shown cheering whilst waving small paper flags depicting the Faraglione family standard, whilst Diva Plaistow was depicted with a barrow energetically selling celebratory sardine tablets and fondant fancies to the tumultuous crowd.

Whilst those depicted amongst the fervent onlookers were somewhat concerned at the liberty apparently taken by dear Irene in presuming their consent to the representation of their likeness in this imaginative way, their anxiety was as of nothing compared to Elizabeth and Benjamin Mapp-Flint, who were initially rendered speechless by their depiction.

"She's really gone too far this time," gasped Elizabeth when she had absorbed what was there for all the world to see.

Whilst most of her friends and neighbours waved cheerfully and scattered garlands before the heroic couple, the Mapp-Flints sat on the kerb in a state of dazed inebriation waving half-empty bottles of strong spirits apparently about to be taken into custody by an approaching constable.

A silent vacuum of tension was eventually fractured by tentative applause that swelled to a heartier round with a concertedly robust contribution from Lord Ardingly and Algernon Wyse.

Lucia was somewhat taken aback by the bemused response of her guests.

Instead of the delight and gleeful appreciation she had anticipated, the initial response had reflected a shock tinged with disbelief, albeit soon submerged in polite applause and compliments expected of guests in genteel society, a least whilst in public.

"Ladies and gentlemen, may I introduce to you my personal gift to Inspector Morrison to thank him not only for his dedicated and brilliant career at the helm of the forces of law and order in our dear Tilling but also for the support he has steadfastly given to me in bearing the many burdens of office as your Mayor and Chief Magistrate over many years."

As the applause following the Mayor's remarks abated, Algernon Wyse felt obliged to fill the awkward silence as the guests struggled to devise appropriate comments to make about the work before them," Quite remarkable, Your Worship," he exclaimed, "What an original piece of work. I can honestly say I have never seen anything quite like it. The audacious composition and technique leads me to wonder if we all might be familiar with the artist responsible. Might I hazard a guess that the painter is known both locally and nationally?"

"Come on Algernon old boy; do spit it out!" boomed a voice from the back of the Garden Room, "Of course it's one of mine. Who else could our brilliant and generous Mayor think of commissioning to celebrate the career of Tilling's very own Inspector Morrison than Tilling's very own Royal Academician, painter extraordinaire and lately rightly garlanded for the Picture of the Year? Moi!"

"Thank you Irene," interrupted Lucia, "I was about to explain that I wished to pay due tribute to the Inspector's triumphant career in Tilling by arranging for our very own brilliant Miss Coles to sum up, to encapsulate so to speak, my productive working relationship with 'my Inspector' in her inimitable style. I do hope that you will agree that Miss Coles has succeeded fulfilling her brief in every material particular?"

By now Elizabeth Mapp-Flint had recovered some semblance of composure and rose to her feet with as much dignity as she could summon, "Lulu, dear one, I'm sure I speak for many present here tonight who are anxious to join with you in thanking our Inspector Morrison for his invaluable service over many years and to wish him well in all his future endeavours in London"

"Hear, hear, my dear!" added Major Benjy, who now had delightedly secured sole access to a decanter of brandy and was making rapid inroads.

"However, dear friend, even you must admit that no-one else featured in this monstrous cartoon of a painting was in any way consulted or even aware of a brief given to Miss Coles?"

"Hard cheese Mapp!" interjected Irene, who by now was sharing the Major's decanter, "I am an artist and feel no obligation to consult or obtain the prior approval of the Grundy's of Tilling"

"Now, now Miss Coles, that is somewhat harsh!" admonished Algernon Wyse, ever the peace-maker.

"Come off it, Algernon, you can't rewrite history. You remember the response to my "Stoning of St Lucia." It was my masterpiece and ended up being slashed to ribbons, partly because it upset so many of you."

"But mainly because your maid Lucy went off her rocker," suggested Diva Plaistow sarcastically.

"You have to admit you people have always feared and ridiculed my work because it shows Tilling as it really is, even my Picture of the Year."

"But how can you say we didn't like it; we went to see it when it was exhibited at the Royal Academy in London?" asked Elizabeth

"Twice!" added Benjy.

"You never stopped complaining until the picture was famous and made you well known. Then you were always posing in front of it for photos and were never out of the newspapers that summer."

"That was entirely another matter, Irene," sniffed Elizabeth, "How can you expect a longtime resident of Tilling, an elected councillor and current Mayoress to react to be being depicted with her husband, a distinguished retired army officer, both roaring drunk, literally sitting in the gutter and about to be arrested? I call it criminal slander and libel. I shall be consulting my solicitor tomorrow and will certainly sue."

"Put a sock in it Mapp, you old bore," shouted Irene, "An artist must go where her muse leads her. That's what I've done and you Philistines must lump it."

"I haven't come here to be insulted Miss Coles" replied Elizabeth with as much dignity as she could muster, "Come Benjy, let us return to Grebe."

Helpless in the face of this sad climax to the proceedings, the hostess, guests of honour and others could only watch in silence as the Mapp-Flints exited the Garden Room and melted into the Sussex night - to the extent that such substantial corporeal frames could "melt" anywhere.

Following this dramatic departure, Lucia turned to her guests and suggested lightly, "Ladies and gentlemen, perhaps we might resume? Now, where were we? Oh, yes, I think Inspector Morrison might wish to say a few words to bring our evening to a close? Inspector…"

Whilst the exchanges had continued between the evening's main protagonists, Herbert and Bunty Morrison had gazed with undisguised horror at the freshly varnished and framed tableau standing on its easel in the window of the Garden Room.

A silent conversation took place between them involving widening of eyes, furrowing of brows, shaking of heads and shrugging of shoulders by which only the closest and most knowing of life partners can communicate with precision and indeed hold entire conversations.

By the time her husband rose to speak, Bunty Morrison knew exactly what he would have to say,

First, Herbert thanked the mayor and her husband for their spectacular hospitality, "My wife and I are so touched and grateful for your generosity and coming to bid us farewell. We shall never forget our final evening here with you all at Mallards"

"You can say that again," muttered Irene as she drained the last drop from Major's decanter.

The Inspector went on to review some of the major cases in his career and to thank all those who had helped him along the way, many of whom sat before him.

Bringing his speech to a close, he thanked both the Mayor and Miss Coles for the "stunning portrait", "I can honestly say it's quite unique. I am deeply honoured and touched to be depicted 'in tandem' so to speak with Mrs Pillson with whom I have had the pleasure and privilege of collaborating so closely and for so long."

Upon these words Lucia smiled graciously and bowed her head in simple acknowledgement.

Simultaneously Herbert directed a meaningful look and raised eyebrow at his wife who nodded discreetly and shot back an even more meaningful glance.

Thus authorised, Herbert continued "Of course, the sheer size, virtuosity and historic significance of the Mayor's most generous and precious gift makes it impractical and inappropriate to think even for a moment to selfishly keep the picture for our own personal enjoyment in our home."

"Absolutely, dear" added Bunty, almost too enthusiastically.

"Accordingly, I would humbly and gratefully ask Mrs Pillson to retain and safeguard Miss Coles' masterpiece in Tilling to be treasured and enjoyed by the people of our historic town for generations to come. Both Bunty and I were born and bred in Tilling and will be comforted in coming years away from our birthplace to think that something of us remains with you."

The Inspector's proposal was received with tumultuous applause and the confident assumption that a suitable place of honour could be found for the masterwork to be displayed in the Town Hall, where it could be enjoyed in perpetuity.

In the black police Riley, on the way back to spend their a final night at 9 Undercliff Villas just outside Tilling before moving to London, Herbert and Bunty Morrison reviewed the events of the evening.

It was agreed that dinner had been sumptuous and so typically generous of the Mayor and that the speeches of thanks and appreciation had been sincere and touching.

Inevitably, conversation turned to the Mayor's farewell gift of the mammoth painting by Irene Coles.

Years of intimacy, mutual understanding and an innate tact had enabled the couple to develop an abbreviated form of communication or shorthand that meant true feelings to be put on record in a minimum of words.

"It was far too large to put up at home, don't you think, Bunty?"

"Oh yes dear, whatever would people have thought?

"Absolutely, after all, I'm not Herr Hitler or Signor Mussolini."

"And it would certainly have given the children nightmares."

CHAPTER TWO:
BEATING THE BOUNDS

CHAPTER TWO

BEATING THE
BOUNDS

A s roseate dawn broke the morning after the Mayor's farewell dinner for Inspector Morrison, a palpable sense of expectancy seemed to hang over the ancient red-roofed town.

As a large pantechnicon loaded with the earthly goods of the Morrison family pulled away from the semi-detached house, 9 Undercliff Villas, Herbert Morrison closed and locked the front door, walked down the front path. After one last glance over his shoulder, he closed the garden gate next to an estate agent's "Sold" sign.

Inspector Morrison joined his wife Bunty and twin children James and Dorothy who awaited him in the black police Riley and drove off to begin a new life and career in London.

At Mallards the Mayor's farewell gift to her now-departed Inspector still stood in the bay window of the Garden Room where it had caused so much heated argument during the previous evening.

Maids Foljambe and Grosvenor exchanged silent but meaningful glances regarding the controversial artwork which rested on its easel again shrouded and protected from public gaze by its sheet, held in place by a gilded rope and tassel.

Neither servant admired the painting and still less the ill-feeling which it had incited, but tact and experience prevented them from venturing any opinion in public.

Their sympathies lay entirely with Mr and Mrs Pillson, their employers of many years. As consummate professionals they simply regretted that the dinner which they had tried so hard to make impeccable had been torn asunder and subverted by yet another very public falling-out involving initially the Mapp-Flints and Irene Coles and by degrees the hostess and several other prominent guests.

At Grebe, some distance outside the venerable walls of Tilling history repeated itself as the atmosphere in the dining room was frosty.

Benjamin Mapp-Flint's attempt to conceal himself behind his "Daily Mirror" as his wife sat down at the breakfast table was doomed from the outset.

"Well?" asked Elizabeth with a sharpness and volume that did not augur well for her husband's well-being and perhaps his safety that day.

"Good morning my dear, 'Well' what?," he replied gamely, if unwisely.

"You know very well what I mean, you drunken dolt," she hissed, with eyes bulging like a King Cobra about to strike, "How can you possibly justify your behaviour last night?"

"I just enjoyed a jolly good dinner, Elizabeth, that's all" he replied plaintively, recognising the hopelessness of his position.

"For the umpteenth time, as soon as you cross the threshold of Mallards, you show me up horribly. You drink far too much of everything in sight, you gush to that woman about her expensive food and drink and never for once stand up for me or support me. You only ever think of yourself and your own pleasure," she continued remorselessly, "In the meantime you desert me completely and leave me completely alone to stand up against constant libel and slander by that woman and her court painter."

"But, Elizabeth," stuttered Benjy, failing completely to stem the flow of vitriol directed at him.

"Not another word, Benjy. You need to understand; you really have gone too far this time. I suggest you get out of my sight, whilst I decide what must be done."

"But Elizabeth, my breakfast!" protested Benjy.

"I'm surprised after last night that you can think of eating or drinking anything," she snorted derisively, "I suggest you make yourself scarce. You can call for a tray later if you really have the nerve. You are entirely worthless and a Judas. Now get out of my sight."

Even by the combative standards of Elizabeth Mapp-Flint, this morning's recriminations had been exceptionally rancorous and bitter.

Benjamin Mapp-Flint was utterly cowed and defeated and exited the dining room without a further word.

Several miles away the breakfast table at Mallards was quiet and somewhat pensive.

Georgie and Lucia Pillson were satisfied that they had acquitted themselves as hosts impeccably. Their guests' every need was accommodated and dinner had been delightful and enjoyed by all.

Both were however profoundly troubled over the spat that had flared up into a massive contretemps between Elizabeth and Irene.

The evening had undoubtedly descended into a virtual brawl with lightening speed, "And all this in front of Lord and Lady Ardingly," sighed Lucia, "I still don't really understand what happened. I thought everyone would be delighted by Irene's painting. Now, I'm not even really sure that inspector Morrison liked it.

"You might be right Lucia," agreed Georgie, "I think it's time we learned some lessons about our friends, don't you?"

""What do you suggest Georgie?" asked Lucia, suspecting that she had drawn the same conclusions from the fiasco.

"Some things definitely must be avoided. We must try not to allow Benjy to drink too much. It always infuriates Elizabeth and make her impossible to deal with."

"Absolutely, Georgie. The same applies to Irene. She must not be allowed too much alcohol; she becomes far too aggressive and outspoken in drink."

"To be honest you cannot afford to commission her again. Her work is too controversial and upsets too many people. You cannot have her more outlandish views attributed to you."

"Even though she adores me absolutely and I agree with her assessment of most people - especially me!"

"Yes, Lucia, and most importantly you must never allow Elizabeth and Irene to enter into mortal combat under your roof. You will always be blamed for their excesses."

"Grazie molto, Georgino mio," replied Lucia, "Oo', molto saggio - or is it sapiente? Now I suppose I need to do something to calm things down after all the unpleasantness last night. I imagine Elizabeth is seething this morning"

"Yes, I would hate to be in Benjy's shoes. Poor man."

"I think I will pop down to the High Street shortly to gauge which way the wind is blowing amongst our guests. In the meantime, perhaps a little Scarlatti to soothe our nerves?"

"Perfecto, Lucia mia."

The morning parliament outside the shops in the High Street was a longstanding tradition in Tilling.

In front of Twistevant's store, Algernon and Susan Wyse stopped to pass the time of day with the Padre and Evie Bartlett. After initial greetings, conversation naturally turned to a review of the events of the previous evening.

"Delightful repast, as ever," remarked Algernon.

"Such a shame it had to end as it did," added Evie.

"Miss Coles seems to feel compelled to sail close to the wind with her paintings," commented Susan Wyse, "I have to say I found her depiction of Algernon and myself verged upon the impertinent."

"Aye tis true, Maistress Wyse," agreed the Padre in Caledonian vein, " Being seen in sacred vestments dementedly spraying Holy Water hither and thither is hardly seemly for an ordained Minister of the Church"

"Or his wife!" squeaked Evie.

"Mind you, our woes are of nothing compared to the humiliation heaped upon our guid friends, the Mapp-Flints."

"You are quite right, Padre, Miss Coles does seem to reserve an especially savage part of her artistic vision to depict Elizabeth and Major Benjy. Each painting seems to represent them in an even worse light than before."

"And poor Elizabeth overreacts every time," said Susan

"Just as Irene wants," suggested Evie, "It's like pouring petrol onto a fire; it just explodes and things soon get out of hand."

"Very embarrassing for our dear hostess," sympathised Algernon Wyse, " I'm sure her motives were of the best and typically generous in commissioning the work in tribute to her relationship with Inspector Morrison."

"But after all these years, she must have known that Irene could only be relied upon to produce work which was guaranteed to infuriate Elizabeth," added Susan, "With the sad results we witnessed last night."

"And this morning Tilling is in shock and waiting to see what Elizabeth will do next and how Irene will respond and what on earth Lucia will do with that unnerving painting," concluded Algernon.

◆ ◆ ◆

As the conversation paused at a convenient juncture after all the implications of the confrontations of the previous evening had been comprehensively analysed, Lucia joined the group.

The empty wicker basket over her arm signified that the Mayor was present to gather intelligence rather than buy groceries.

After the usual round of greetings, inquiries as to well-being and hat-doffing, Lucia inquired , "Any news."

Unusually, this produced a degree of discomfort since the only news of the day would be the fall-out from last night's confrontation and the chief protagonists had yet to surface.

Discerning only manifest unease and that there was little yet to be learned but much damage to repair to the social fabric at the apogee of Tilling society, Lucia decided to move on for now. She would return to the fray when circumstances were more promising and conducive to constructive manipulation..

"Well dear friends. I must rush I'm afraid," said Lucia gaily, "By the way Padre, could you possibly spare me a minute or two this afternoon?"

"Of course, Your Worship," he replied, "'There is always time in my busy schedule for the important affairs of Church and State."

"Thank you, Padre. Perhaps you could join me at Mallards House for tea at four?"

As the Mayor walked back to Mallards with her still-empty basket, the group exchanged quizzical glances questioning the import of the pending church-state summit. This would no doubt emerge at their next pavement parliament.

As the clock in the Norman tower of St Mary's church chimed four that afternoon, Grosvenor showed the Padre into the Garden Room where Lucia and a fully laden tea table awaited, "Reverend Bartlett, Ma'am."

"Thank you Grosevenor. I will attend to tea " said Lucia inviting her visitor to sit. May I pour some tea, Padre? Do help yourself to a sandwich."

As ever, the Padre needed no encouragement to enjoy the abundance of finger sandwiches, scones and fancies on the silver stand before him."

As they enjoyed their refreshments, conversation touched upon many issues, ranging from health to the weather, British Summertime and the uncertain international political climate.

Neither the Padre nor his hostess found it necessary to raise the spectre of the more controversial aspects of the previous evening and confined themselves to praising the splendid catering and regret the departure from Tilling of its distinguished senior police officer.

When they had begun their second cup of tea, Lucia moved on the the real businesss of the day, "Now Padre, I wanted to discuss with you a proposal that has been on my mind for some time. The idea occurred to me following a very interesting meeting with my Town Clerk. He showed to me some of our older civic records detailing various ancient customs that have fallen into desuetude in the current century."

"Och aye, Maistess Pillson, there are certainly a lot of traditions we nae longer follow in Tilling: the stocks and ducking stool for instance."

"Fear not Padre, I am not going to suggest that we bring back either or public flogging," joked Lucia, "Although after last night, I do sometimes wonder."

"Probably for the best, your Worship," said the Padre with a smile, "What are you thinking of reviving?"

"I don't know if you have ever heard of the ancient ritual of Beating the Bounds, Padre? I looked it up in Chambers 'Book of

Days' and it says the custom had two aims: first, 'to supplicate Divine Blessing on the fruits of the earth' and secondly, 'to preserve in all classes of the community correct knowledge of and respect for the bounds of parochial property.'"

"I have a vague recollection of the practice," admitted the Padre, "I think the official term for the procession was a 'perambulation'? But I don't recall it ever taking place in any of my parishes in the past. What are you suggesting Mrs Pillson?"

"Well Padre, I think it behoves us all to treasure and nurture local history and practices for the benefit of future generations."

"Indeed, Your Worship"

"And though I do not want to dwell unduly on commerce and issues of Mammon, I think my proposal might well boost the economy of the town. The historic points of difference between our beloved Tilling and surrounding towns all increase its appeal to visitors and add to the tourist trade upon which so many businesses here depend."

"That is undeniable, Mrs Pillson. And would you be wanting to involve both the Church and Town Council?"

"I think so, Padre. In many locations I gather that a group of local people including the Vicar, parish elders, Mayor and councillors and children would process around the parish boundaries. The elders would point out the extent of the boundaries by identifying certain trees, marker stones and field corners. And the younger members of the village would be expected to remember those boundary markers to ensure that there was a collective memory"

"Oh I see. It must all be very colourful. No wonder it attracts tourists," enthused then Padre.

"It also has a lighter side Padre. At set points during the perambulation as well as prayers at locations like 'Gospel Oak' and 'Amen Corner', there were often celebratory refreshments, a 'drinking together of ale' and consumption of cakes and cheese."

"In the procession," continued Lucia, "willow wands were usually carried by adults and children to physically beat the boundary markers. To encourage youngsters to remember these key locations, the information was sometimes beaten into them and the practice developed of beating boys with sticks or even tipping them upside down and banging heads on the stones. This bizarre ritual came to be known as 'bumping.'"

"I don't think we want any bumping of our wee folk in Tilling, do we, Worship?" asked the Padre.

"Certainly not, Padre, but I would like to involve as many of our community as possible and to make the event as colourful and interesting as we can manage. If it happens to feature on the newsreels in the cinemas and encourage visitors to Tilling so much the better."

"Aye, Mrs Pillson, I'm sure our shopkeepers and Chamber of Commerce would be delighted."

"I remember when Pathe News featured our successful Elizabethan Pageant in dear Riseholme, they had to organise special trains and charabancs from Birmingham and the local economy benefited immensely."

"That sounds very promising Mrs Pillson. I see no reason why the parish and council should not cooperate to revive this ancient tradition in Tilling. With Rogation-tide approaching I had better seek permission from the Bishop and perhaps you will open discussions with the Council?"

"Of course, Padre, may I pour some more tea."

In the succeeding days the Mayor and Padre busied themselves in bringing about revival of Beating the Bounds in Tilling.

The Padre attended at the Diocesan Office and requested initial permission to bring back the ritual.

The Bishop required to discuss the proposals personally with the Padre and, after forensic analysis, had no objection. The episcopal view was that revived practice would make a positive contribution to increasing the profile of the church in the district and increase community involvement in its activities.

The Padre was left to liaise with the Mayor and his own lay deacons, wardens and congregation regarding the modern format of the ceremonial and its implementation.

For the Mayor, once diocesan approval had been given, the process of actioning civic involvement was more straightforward.

Her first task was to gain full council approval for the revival of the ceremony.

The Mayor described the proposed event to the Council as a cooperative venture between the parish of St Mary in Tilling and the civil authority, "A revival of Beating the Bounds would stimulate interest in the glorious medieval history of our town and also add to its profile as a charming attraction for visitors."

"The Beating the Bounds will also present an opportunity to present modern Tilling in the very best light," added the Mayor, "Given the size of the parish and it's lengthy boundaries, there is planned to be a colourful initial procession of the entire Corporation from the Town Hall to St Mary's Church for prayers and a blessing from the Padre with accompaniment of sacred music from the choir."

After the odd "Hear, hear" from loyalist councillors and a pronounced stony silence from her Mayoress and usual opponents such as Councillor Twistevant, the Mayor continued, "The participants in the ceremonial beating shall proceed in a stately progress to the five or six key locations on the margin of the parish where the boundary will be established, declared and, in fact, physically beaten with authentic willow wands in accordance with medieval precedent. I am pleased to report that the Tilling Wheelers and local Boy Scouts and Girl Guides have agreed to accompany the Official Bound Beating party on bicycles to expedite the progress of the ritual."

"And will Your Worship, employ the famed Mayoral tandem as she peddles from one point to another?" asked Elizabeth Mapp-Flint, slyly referring to the recent controversial painting depicting the Mayor and her departed Police Inspector.

" I think Councillor Mapp-Flint may be confusing art with reality," suggested Lucia sweetly, "If the proposed ceremonial revival is approved, I intend to use my own bicycle - the one that I have enjoyed riding in and around Tilling for many years past.

"And may we take it that the recommencement of this pagan rite will not involve beating, bumping or the infliction of injury upon the young folk of the parish?" added Elizabeth somewhat mischievously. "Your Worship may recall the various cases of second and third degree burns inflicted upon several children scrambling for heated pennies when this dangerous rite of pelting the junior citizens of the town with superheated coinage from the balcony of the King's Arms was revived by her some years ago? Sadly, it resulted in several civil actions against the Council for substantial damages for personal injury."

"Yes, I can confirm that what I believe is called 'bumping' or any other such attack on the person has been entirely expunged from the rites to be re-enacted and the revitalised Beating of the Bounds in Tilling will not involve any threat whatsoever to any minor or indeed adult member of the parish," answered Lucia wearily, "Now that we have addressed this important point, may I commend this imaginative proposal to the Council and ask for its approval?"

Assent was duly given, leaving the Mayor to resolve logistics with her Town Clerk and the heads of relevant municipal departments.

At the same meeting, the Council also formally noted the recent generous long-term loan from its former distinguished senior police officer, Inspector Sir Herbert Morrison of a full length ceremonial portrait featuring both the Inspector and Mayor amongst the people of Tilling.

In keeping with usual procedure, it was resolved that the offer and issues of acceptance and future display should be deferred to the standing civic artwork sub committee chaired by the Mayoress whose decision would be reported back to council in due course.

The Council also noted that the Inspector had recently left his post as senior officer with Tilling Police to take up the position of Assistant Commissioner of the Metroploitan Police in London.

The sincere thanks of the Council for the Inspector's valued service to the town and good wishes for his future career were duly expressed by unanimous vote and minuted.

The Mayor was able to achieve her aim of reviving Beating the Bounds in short order by convening a committee in which all relevant departments were represented and closely managing the process until her plan was implemented precisely as she had wished.

As a result of the combined efforts and concerted will of the Padre and Mayor, a detailed plan to revive the ancient ritual was in place within ten days of the proposal first being mooted.

CHAPTER THREE:
A NEAR-DEATH
EXPERIENCE

Chapter Three

**A Near-death
Experience**

M eaning "asking," Rogation was traditionally a season for solemn supplication for the blessing of God on crops and animals.

From the seventeenth century, rogationtide was marked in Sussex and elsewhere by the colourful custom of beating the bounds at which parish boundaries were traversed and energetically swatted with wands of vegetation.

This was supposed to assist in committing the borders to common memory and was said often to be combined with bouncing children off stone markers and consuming considerable quantities of strong ale and sweetmeats in celebration.

Under the benign rule of its Mayor and with the benefit of the spiritual guidance of its Padre, however, Tilling did not plan to reintroduce the enforced public concussion of minors.

In truth the ancient Cinque port needed little encouragement to process and undertake elaborate public ritual in all its civic and ecclesiastical finery.

This was particularly the case when press photographers and newsreel cinematographers were present to record and publicise the event.

As planned, the day on which Tilling's bounds were to be beaten began with a stately progress by the entire Corporation from the steps of there town hall around surrounding streets to St Mary's Church where the Vicar, Reverent Bartlett and his choristers awaited.

The procession was headed by the Town Clerk in formal dress bearing the bejewelled antique mace of the Corporation, sparkling in the sunshine.

The Mayor in formal attire including her tricorn hat, chain of office and ermine-trimmed robe was accompanied by the alderman and councillors of the borough.

The processing councillors waved cheerfully to the applauding onlookers made up of citizens and visitors to the town.

On arrival at St Mary's, the vicar made a brief address of welcome followed by prayers, a blessing and an invitation to join in several hymns generally considered to be of an encouraging nature beginning with "Fight the good fight" leading onto "Onwards Christian Soldiers."

With a parting blessing, the Mayor, Town Clerk and selected Councillors were joined by a contingent of the Tilling Wheelers in their formal society wear of badged blazer and tassled peaked cap on bicycles in an orderly procession down through the Landgate and ancient walls of the town to the open road below.

The more dextrous Wheelers managed to process upon their bicycles whilst holding wands of willow and other assorted vegetation with which to assail bounds and other strategic points on various parish boundaries during the planned rituals.

As the civic and ecclesiastical party peddled away most onlookers applauded enthusiastically.

Characteristically, the lone voice of Elizabeth Mapp-Flint adopted a more cynical tone, "As her Mayoress, I am obliged to go along with this latest stunt by dear Lulu, but honestly," she railed, "Why we have to go through this Ruritanean nonsense is quite beyond me: pure ostentation. I just don't see the point of the whole Council and our Padre pedalling sweatily around the parish armed with sticks and singing hymns just to hit random walls and bouncing unwary children off stones and such. It's all pagan gobbledegook to me."

Evie Bartlett and Diva Plaistow listened in cowed silence. After Elizabeth's recent spectacular tirade at Mallards, both knew that given her mood just now any attempt at contradiction was pointless.

Relishing this absence of resistance, Elizabeth ploughed remorselessly on, "Still, dearest Lulubelle gets her picture in the paper again and has fun making a spectacle of herself riding that terrible old boneshaker of hers in full fig, so I suppose, as always, we will all just have to put up with it. I think it's unseemly and undignified - especially for a woman of her age!"

◆ ◆ ◆

Ninety minutes or so later, the first two bounds on the itinerary had been successfully beaten and the process marked with prayers, a hymn and blessing plus several press photographs including an ingenious grouping of several rows of waving participants sitting on bicycles photographed from above with the help of a stepladder.

After two stops for refreshments, the more boisterous members of the Tilling Wheelers had enjoyed surprisingly copious quantities of the celebratory strong ale served.

One or two Wheelers deplored the failure to follow long established tradition and felt the urge to revive the custom of bouncing a young parishioner on each boundary marker stone.

Despite the express instruction and indeed prohibition of both the Mayor and Reverend Bartlett, they were determined that the practice of bouncing local juveniles to ensure the bounds were fully and memorably beaten and absorbed within the communal memory would be energetically revived.

The first unfortunate youth selected for this honour was the head chorister from St Mary's.

An extremely unwilling participant in the ritual, the shy and studious youth was reluctantly captured by several muscular Wheelers, brusquely inverted and, in keeping with ancient practice, enthusiastically bounced upon a venerable granite marker close to Camber Castle.

Loud mirth accompanied this swift and dramatic manhandling.

Fortunately no blood was spilled or bones broken in the process, but the unhappy bouncee was concussed in the process and, when eventually released, tottered away from the scene of his assault dazed and possibly mentally scarred for life.

Nearby. Lucia was discussing with the Padre the next location to be visited for the penultimate Beating of the day.

Noticing the hubbub around the boundary marker both recognised what was going on and shouted at the errant Wheelers to stop at once.

Furious that her express instructions had been ignored so blatantly, Lucia pedalled at speed towards the group, shouting, "Stop it this instant. You must not do that to the poor child!"

The delinquent Wheelers stood back sheepishly as the Mayor flew towards them.

Unfortunately, in her haste the ermine trim of her robe caught in the chain of her bicycle, bringing it to an immediate uncontrolled halt.

As a result, proceeded by her heavy gilded chain of office, gleaming in the sunshine, the Mayor of Tilling flew at remarkable speed headlong in a dramatic arc over the handlebars.

As the Mayoral tricorn hat floated through the air to the turf on the nearby verge, the Mayor hit the ground with alarming force and her head struck the granite boundary marker with what onlooker later described to a reported from the "Tilling Gazette" as "a sickening thud."

Immediately afterwards all was silent, save for the metallic clicking of a still-rotating bicycle wheel and distant birdsong.

As her once pristine bicycle lay on the tarmac, scratched and dented by the impact, Lucia lay motionless with a trickle of blood running down her uncreased forehead.

After what seemed a long and unreal silence that in reality only lasted seconds, the horror of what had taken place dawned on bystanders.

"Call an ambulance!" shouted the Padre rushing to the Mayor's side.

As a church warden of many years standing, Dr Dobbie was fortunately present for the ceremony and was able to hasten to Lucia's prone body. He placed the Mayor in what he termed "the recovery position" and checked her pulse.

"Is she breathing, Doctor?"asked the Padre anxiously, for once foreswearing any regional accent and speaking the plainest of English.

"Yes, but unconscious." he replied.

An ambulance attended promptly and with bells ringing rushed the still unconscious Mayor to Tilling Cottage Hospital for urgent treatment.

Georgie Pillson was called to his wife's bedside as many friends from the town waited anxiously for news.

Within hours, Tilling was awash with rumour and conjecture about what had taken place and the condition of the Mayor.

All too soon, Dr Dobbie stood outside the Mayor's hospital room to brief concerned neighbours on her condition. "I'm afraid I do not have a great deal to say," he explained, "Mrs Pillson suffered a sharp blow to her forehead colliding with a stone marker as a result of her accident and possible a cranial fracture, following which she lost consciousness. Although her vital signs are stable, she has not yet come round. We will be conducting further tests and will continue observe the patient's condition closely."

"So does that mean Lucia is in a coma?" asked Georgie with concern.

"I'm afraid it does, Mr Pillson."

"And when will she come round, Doctor?"

"I'm afraid it's too early to say as yet, but rest assured that we will do everything possible to make her comfortable and stable in the meantime. I'm afraid all we can do for now is monitor and wait."

CHAPTER FOUR: A VERY TILLING COUP

CHAPTER FOUR

A VERY TILLING
COUP

A fter his wife's admission to Tilling Cottage Hospital, Georgie Pillson maintained a constant vigil by her bedside.

Predictably, Lucia's most devoted admirer Irene Coles, was beside herself with anxiety following the injury to the person she adored above all others.

Following Lucia's admission, Irene waited for news outside her room. At night when asked to leave the premises, Irene maintained a solitary vigil in the street outside lighting candles and sending positive thoughts to her patron and inspiration with only occasional breaks to return to Taormina to change or respond to the occasional calls from nature.

As each hour passed, there was no alteration in the patient's condition. The only change evident was the regular arrival of deliveries from all over the globe.

Flowers, telegrams and baskets of fruit arrived from Lucia's many distinguished friends.

A case of vintage champagne was accompanied by a touching handwritten note of support from famous operatic diva and friend Olga Bracely.

The Cont and Contessa di Faraglione sent fresh honey, peaches and wine from Capri with heartfelt good wishes and an invitation to recuperate on their sunny isle at the earliest opportunity.

The uniformed chauffeur of Lord Ardingly delivered a large wicker basket of the choicest orchids personally selected by her Ladyship from the hothouses at Ardingly with a personal handwritten note.

As Lord Lieutenant of the County, he felt able to add to the good wishes of himself and Lady Ardingly, those of their Majesties who had been delighted so recently to confer upon her the well deserved honour and dignity of Damehood.

The perfume of roses and orchids filled Lucia's hospital room and brightly coloured cards filled every available surface and soon spilled out to the corridor outside.

A succession of friends and neighbours called to inquire about progress and left disappointed to hear that Mrs Pillson remained unconscious but was receiving constant care.

As might be expected in Tilling, conjecture continued to mount as each day went by without any change.

Talk during marketing in the High Street, after church on Sunday morning and over tea and bridge at Diva Plaistow's concerned only Lucia's condition.

Much irritation was directed towards the boorish element amongst the Tilling Wheelers who were widely felt to be responsible for the Mayor's terrible injury because they had drunkenly taken it upon themselves to bounce Tilling's leading chorister so brutally on an ancient boundary marker of the hardest granite.

It was understood that twins Georgie and Per, the joint Chairman of Tilling Wheelers - as well as virtually every other sporting association in the town - had visited their Life President in her bed of pain to apologise personally for the unforgivable part played by an unruly element in their organisation in the dreadful accident.

The guilty parties had been reprimanded, banished from the Club and stripped of their tasselled Wheelers caps. Sadly the brothers had been obliged to leave their sincere letter of apology by the bedside unread since the victim had not yet recovered consciousness.

It was learned that the irate father of the concussed chorister had complained to the police about the common assault upon his son and heir. It was generally hoped that criminal charges would ensue and that justice would be done.

Whilst her doctors puzzled as to how to bring Lucia back to consciousness, civic life continued.

In the Council House, Elizabeth Mapp-Flint knocked upon the door of the office of Mr Temple, the Town Clerk and bustled in.

Suspecting something was afoot Mr Temple stood up from his desk and greeted his visitor, "Good morning Mrs Mapp-Flint, what can I do for you?"

Elizabeth wasted no time in outlining her concerns and several very specific questions.

She soon ascertained that a town by-law passed in the reign of George III provided that whilst the Mayor was indisposed, the Mayoress or any other Councillor authorised by due majority of the Council could deputize and exercise all the powers and prerogatives of the Mayor including a casting vote in the event of equality or deadlock.

He also confirmed that the art sub committee delegated to act by the full Council had full powers to determine the matters referred to it, subject always to proper contrary vote of the full Council.

The Mayoress reviewed with the Clerk forthcoming scheduled business and the procedure to be followed to put forward measures of her own for consideration.

Hitherto whilst Lucia presided over proceedings, Elizabeth had little opportunity to promote her own agenda and was mainly occupied in fruitless opposition of Lucia's programme or complaining when it was implemented, as it invariably seemed to be the case.

As she departed Elizabeth thanked the Clerk for his advice and thought to herself, "Things are going to be a bit different in Tilling now. Just you wait Your Worship!"

From the Town Hall, the Mayoress walked briskly to Twistevant's, the grocers in the High Street.

Asking if Mr Twistevant was available, she was shown into the small dark office behind the shop. There at his desk sat Councillor Harold Twistevant counting the days takings.

"Thank you for sparing me a moment, Mr Twistevant," said Elizabeth.

"Time you called me 'Harold', don't you think; we've known each other for years"

"Er, thank you...Harold," she replied hesitantly.

"Now, what can I do for you, Elizabeth?"

"More what I can do for you really," she replied, as close to being coy as her formidable matronly persona could manage, "Now that our poor Mayor is incommoded, it falls to us as her remaining colleagues to ensure that the affairs of the Council run, shall we say, 'smoothly'"

"Exactly how 'smoothly' do you mean?" asked Mr Twistevant, intrigued.

"As you know, our political agenda has not always corresponded with the Mayor's."

"You can say that again," replied Mr Twistevant, "She seems to have made it her business to ruin me. Look at her attack on my picturesque residences down by the station. She plans to take them from me and demolish the lot of them."

"I think the Mayor said they were 'slums, unfit for human habitation' and that you would be 'compensated in accordance with the law' when they're compulsorily acquired."

"Whose side are you on Mrs Mapp-Flint ?" he asked, frostily.

"I am on the side of the good people of Tilling, of course, including you," she said with the toothiest of smiles, in an effort to reassure her potential ally, "Now let me tell you what I have in mind"

"Go on then."

"The Town Clerk advises me that whilst our Mayor is hors de combat.."

"Hors de what?"

"Unconscious and unable to do anything"

"Oh..carry on."

"I can deputise as Mayor and, if my arithmetic is right, use the votes on the Council you control and if necessary my casting vote to ensure whatever measures I - or rather 'we' - want are passed,"

"Oh I see, so my historic cottages so convenient for the railway station need not be demolished?"

"Indeed, Harold," smiled Elizabeth.

"And if you don't mind me asking, what's in it for you ?"

"Obviously, as a good citizen I simply want to do what is right and benefits the good folk of Tilling."

"Especially if it annoys Lucia?" said Mr Twistevant, winking.

"I couldn't possibly comment," replied the Mayoress, "But I'm sure there will be a number of projects on which we will be able to co-operate in the public interest."

"Oh, I see," he enthused, "A 'you scratch my back' sort of arrangement?"

"If you want to put it like that, I suppose so. Anyway, I've taken up quite enough of your time for today. When you receive the agenda for the next meeting of the Council, you will appreciate the items of, shall we say, 'mutual interest'. I suggest we liaise nearer the time to ensure that the correct decisions are made?"

"Very well, that's a deal. Good day, Elizabeth."

"Good day, Harold."

◆ ◆ ◆

Each passing day, seemed an age as Lucia remained unconscious.

DERYCK J. SOLOMON

Ever her devoted cavalier serviente, Georgie Pillson sat quietly by her bedside.

Several specialists travelled down from London to assess the patient.

After various reviving drugs failed to achieve the desired effect, doctors tried other stimulants to return Lucia to consciousness. A gramophone was brought to the bedside and recordings played at various volumes in an effort to bring about a response.

An favourite aria by Olga Braceley from Cortese's "Lucretia" and even the finest rendition of the slow movement from the Moonlight Sonata failed to elicit any reaction.

As an orderly removed the gramophone, Georgie sighed and looked expectantly at Dr. Dobbie, "What now doctor? Is there anything else we can do? "

"I"m afraid that we have run out of fresh ideas for now, though we will continue to seek expert guidance - even from abroad if necessary. For now I think it is important that you keep trying. I suggest that you continue to talk to your wife. She knows your voice better than anyone's. If anyone can pierce the veil of her coma, it's you. I will leave you both in peace, so you can carry on talking."

"Thank you Doctor," Georgie replied, again taking up Lucia's pale hand, and whispering gently as his wife's head lay still on the Tilling Cottage Hospital-issue pillow.

As the door closed leaving them alone, Georgie commented, "Life is strange Lucia mia, isn't it? In all the time I have known you, we have never ever been this close. It only took a medieval ritual, granite marker and coma to do it."

"Now," he added, "I know you would normally begin with 'Any news?' I have to say there's heaps to catch up on. Everyone in Tilling is very worried about you. They have all inquired every day and sent flowers and cards. As you can imagine Irene is quite hysterical and spends every night on the pavement outside lighting candles and generally being distraught."

Georgie paused and looked closely for any response. Lucia simply breathed and looked expressionless, as though listening to a speech by her Mayoress to the Council about burdensome rates or yet another sermon from the Padre about the ills of British Summertime.

"I'm sorry to tell you that Elizabeth has been up to her old tricks again," he resumed, "It seems she has taken full advantage of your absence by manipulating votes of the Council. She now stands in for you as Mayor and seems to set the agenda. She has formed this alliance with Councillor Twistevant and his cronies and completely quashed your scheme to knock down those terrible slums of his down by the station."

With no response forthcoming, George continued his monologue, "And perhaps worst of all, she has manipulated that art subcommittee she chairs. She wasn't able to get them to reject Inspector Morrison's gift of Irene's portrait with you on the tandem. Much, worse; it was accepted and she arranged for it to be hung at the end of a narrow unlit corridor in the very basement of the Town Hall next to the male maintenance staff lavatory."

With the utterance of the word "lavatory" the fingers of the comatose Mayor tightened perceptibly around those of her husband and for the first time since her roadside trauma, her eyes opened with a kind of shocked bewilderment.

"Doctor! Nurse! Somebody! Anyone!" he shouted, "I think she's come round! Help me!"

CHAPTER FIVE: NORMAL SERVICE IS RESUMED

Chapter Five :
Normal Service is
Resumed

W ord spread rapidly throughout Tilling about the dramatic turn of events in the Cottage Hospital.

"She's back! Our lovely Lucia is safe and well!" exclaimed Irene Coles, literally skipping into the saloon bar of the Traders Arms and calling loudly for the first of many pints of beer in celebration.

Within hours, Lucia was actually sitting up in her hospital bed asked her maid Grosvenor to assist in making her more presentable, so that she might receive visitors.

Georgie Pillson beamed in happiness and relief and warned the patient, "Now Lucia. You heard what Dr Dobbie said. You have been in a coma for a week and really mustn't overdo it now. You may see the Bartletts and Wyses briefly, but then must rest."

For once, the Mayor of Tilling did precisely as she was bidden.

Within days, all required neurological tests, x-rays and blood counts were satisfactorily completed and Lucia was deemed fit to return home.

By this time a large number of her friends and neighbours had called upon the Mayor in her hospital room and her Town Clerk and Tilling's new Senior police officer, Inspector Newman had even been able to take warrants and other official documents to her for signature.

A real sense of occasion prevailed as Lucia was eventually discharged and nurses and other staff formed a line as she shook their hands one by one and shared a personal word of thanks on leaving.

Watching the departure Elizabeth Mapp-Flint muttered under her breath, "You would think it was a Royal Visit. At least the nurses weren't expected to curtsy. Oh, well. I suppose it was nice while it lasted…"

As her hospital room had been, Mallards overflowed with flowers and cards from well-wishers.

Offers of hospitality to recuperate with friends abounded.

Possible destinations varied from the Villa Faraglione in Capri and Olga Bracely's luxurious villa in Le Touquet to Ambermere Hall and Lucia's former home, The Hurst in picturesque Riseholme in Worcestershire.

Before deciding upon her preference, Lucia was determined to restore the rightful order of things in Tilling.

This process effectively involved undoing all the mischief done by her dear friend and loyal Mayoress Elizabeth-Mapp, whilst Lucia was incommoded.

Lucia's grasp of relevant procedural rules and regulations was unparalleled in Tilling and, unlike her Mayoress, she had no need to obtain information or advice from the Town Clerk.

Responding to a note delivered by chauffeur Cadman five minutes before, Councillor and leading businessman, slum landlord and grocer, Harold Twistevant stood at the front door of Mallards.

Shown into the Garden Room, the visitor was soon seated and inquiring about his fellow councillor's health.

Placed as they were at opposite ends of the admittedly narrow political spectrum in Tilling, the Mayor and her visitor had little scope, or indeed inclination, to engage in protracted smalltalk.

Lucia soon seized the initiative, "Thank you for coming so promptly Councillor Twistevant."

"My pleasure, Your worship," he replied, feeling in no way tempted to suggest that they resort to first names.

"I hear that whilst I was, shall we say, 'away', the Council decided to not to proceed with the Compulsory Purchase Order affecting, inter alia, your tenanted residences down by the station."

"Yes it did," he admitted, with a smile somewhere between smug and sheepish.

Within five further minutes Councillor Twistevant had been persuaded to adapt what Lucia described as "a more progressive approach to the amelioration of Tillling's stock of residential housing."

Lucia was pleased to inform her fellow councillor that there appeared to have been a material understatement of the value of his historic cottages and thus the compensation payable.

Furthermore, the Mayor now felt able to disclose that in recognition of his "valued contribution to the civic life of Tilling and the welfare of its citizens over a long career" it was proposed that the new council homes to be built to replace the demolished slums should be called "Twistevant Mansions" in his honour.

In all honesty, Lucia was not entirely certain how she had managed to string together the previous sentence without being struck down by a thunderbolt from on high.

Retaining her composure, she turned to her visitor and inquired, " So, Mr Twistevant, I trust that this development meets with your approval?"

"It certainly does, Your Worship," he enthused, "I will be pleased and honoured to see it proceed."

"Very well, I am happy that you are content," she replied, "And perhaps we can also tidy up a few other 'infelicities' that seem to have cropped up in my absence, don't you think?"

"I don't see why not, Mrs Pillson. I look forward to welcoming you back into the Council Chamber soon."

At the next meeting of the Council, Lucia had resumed her Mayoral chair and conducted proceedings.

The dismay of Elizabeth Mapp-Flint and her faction was palpable when the it was announced that the compulsory purchase and demolition of the slums by the station would now proceed and that the replacement housing should be named after Harold Twistevant.

""What a Judas," Elizabeth hissed in the direction of her smiling former ally, "Should be should be called Turncoat Mansions. It's a disgrace, it really is!"

Her chagrin grew even worse when, the decision of the art sub-committee regarding the positioning of the portrait recently donated by Inspector Morrison was reversed by vote of the full council.

The Mayor was pleased to note that, "the brilliant celebratory masterwork by prominent local artist Miss Irene Coles, RA will now be on permanent display in the Mayor's Parlour here in the Council House where it can be regularly enjoyed by councillors, employees and visitors for years to come."

On receiving this second reverse of the meeting, the face of the Mayoress fell as though a fierce body blow had been followed by a sharp uppercut.

Seeing metaphorical stars, the Mayoress left the Council House at the end of the meeting without uttering a further word. Light rain began to fall as Elizabeth began the long walk out through the Landgate and back towards Grebe.

◆ ◆ ◆

CHAPTER SIX:
LAST LEG

Chapter Six:
Last Leg

C omfortable silence prevailed in the dining room of
Mallards that morning.

It was only a week ago that Georgie and Lucia Pillson had returned from a holiday at the villas of dear friends in Capri and Le Touquet.

There Lucia had convalesced following the head injury suffered whilst reviving the ceremony of Beating the Bounds in Tilling which sadly resulted in a week's loss of consciousness.

Lucia preferred to refer to her "loss of consciousness'" rather than use the term "coma," since she wished to avoid unhelpful conjecture regarding any possible reduction in her mental capacity.

Experience had taught her that certain of her intimes could be relied upon to put such matters in the worst possible light given the slightest excuse.

Pleased to be home, the chatelaine of the double-fronted red brick townhouse from the time of one of the Georges, ate her stewed prunes and scanned the obituary column of her morning broadsheet.

"Oh, dear," she exclaimed, "How very sad!"

"What's that?" replied Georgie, whose primary concern at that moment was the removal of a spot of marmalade that had inconveniently found its way onto his favourite silk tie from Turnbull and Asser, "How very tarsome, it's brand new!"

Oblivious to her life-partner's distress, Lucia explained, "Dead."

Silence reigned as Georgie continued to worry about his neckwear.

"Leg," she continued absently.

"Like in rugger?" asked Georgie

"What do you mean, Georgie?

"It was awfully painful, as I recall. When you got a kick there and then went quite numb. Not that I played often. Terribly rough and far too much mud."

"What on earth are you talking about, dear? "

"You said something about dead legs and I was simply recounting my own limited experience, Lucia."

"No, dear, nothing to do with rugby, 'Susan.' Susan Leg - surely you remember her - wrote romances - it says here 'world-wide novelist' - went under the name 'Rudolf da Vinci?"

"What about her?" asked Georgie, who by now had dipped the corner of his napkin in his water glass and was carefully dabbing his tie.

"Deceased, Georgie dear. Susan is no more. It says here that she passed over 'whilst enjoying a hearty high tea at Fortnum & Mason in Piccadilly."

"Seems rather apt from what I remember," remarked Georgie, "Having seen her work her way through plate after plate of cook's nougat fancies on her visit here, it always seemed possible that it might end unhappily. What that woman could do to a plate of jam doughnuts always beggared belief."

"Not to mention what Elizabeth calls 'those questionable sardine tartlets at Diva's,'" added Lucia.

"Oh, yes, I remember - 'sea food roulette,'" giggled Georgie.

"Still, it is sad that she has passed on."

"Or, as she would no doubt have put it 'passed over to the Other Side and joined the Choir Invisible', "suggested Georgie.

"True. Susan did have a somewhat florid turn of phrase."

"Florid, but so very lucrative."

" I remember her once telling me 'I never take a holiday and shall not rest until the shadows of life's eventide close around me .'"

"I suppose it was the shadow of Fortnum's choux buns and vanilla slices that closed around her? There are worse ways to shuffle off this mortal coil, I suppose," suggested Georgie.

"We must take care not to speak ill of the dead, dear."

"However gluttonous, swanky or verbose,"

"Be that as it may, Georgie, whatever her weaknesses, we should give dear Susan her due. She was after all hugely well-known and successful."

"Judging by the her footman, butler, chauffeur and Daimler, you are quite right. And so you forgive her for eating us out of house and home, boring us to distraction with her imperious ways and generally taking full advantage of our hospitality?"

"Basically, yes, Georgie. You must remember my position in the town. Susan Leg was a distinguished, internationally known author to whom, as Mayor of Tilling, I felt obliged to extend hospitality. My personal connection with this celebrity conferred distinction on our dear Tilling."

"And on its dear Mayor?" teased Georgie.

"Public life behoves one to shoulder many burdens dear one, regardless of one's personal feelings or preferences," drawled Lucia, looking loftily into the middle distance and projecting what she imagined constituted her best patrician profile, "Simply civic duty or perhaps even, 'noblesse oblige'."

"And how is this noblesse now to be demonstrated?"asked Georgie, sensing that life in Tilling was again about to be enlivened by what more cynical Tillingites had long come to describe as "another of Lucia's stunts."

"I think it is about time that I gave another interview to that nice Mr Meriton from the 'Tilling Gazette', don't you think Georgie?"

Several days later out at Grebe on the marshes, its Mayoress Elizabeth Mapp-Flint lunched with her husband Major Benjamin.

Sufficient time had passed since the Major had disgraced himself by drinking to excess at the dinner held at Mallards in honour of the departing senior police officer, Inspector Morrison.

Though not wholly rehabilitated, the guilty party was now allowed to speak to his wife and share meals, though not as yet the marital couch. It was widely reported amongst servants in Tilling that the Major still remained banished to the couch in his dressing room.

As she toyed with her undistinguished macaroni cheese, Elizabeth idly turned the pages of the new edition of the "Tilling Gazette." "Heaven help us, Lulu is up to her old tricks!"she exclaimed.

"What now, Elizabeth?" asked the Major from behind his "Daily Mirror."

"Yet another exclusive interview with that ghastly old hack Meriton. Worship just has to snap her fingers and that inky - fingered sycophant comes running to do her bidding. He's just her lapdog."

"What does she have to say this time?" asked the Major.

"Plus c'est la meme chose, I'm afraid ma cherie. Like always, the poor dolt is kneeling at the feet of the chatelaine of Mallards -' the eternal epicentre of civic and cultural life in Tilling - enjoying the cup that cheers but not inebriates'..."

"Nothing new there then,"said Benjy, who very much preferred a cup that inebriated, "So what does it say she's up to this time?"

"Ah, here it is," explained Elizabeth, "Lulu says she was a long-standing intime of late world-wide novelist Susan Leg, globally known as 'Rudolf da Vinci'. Apparently only she called her by the affectionate name of' 'Susannah'"

"That's not all she called her, if I remember correctly."

"Indeed, Benjy! It seems dear sweet Susannah liked nothing more than to stay with Lulu at Mallards and used to call it her 'home from home'"

"On her one and only visit, you mean?"

"Again, too true, dear. There's more; apparently Worship feels it her duty to share with the readers of the 'Tilling Gazette' her unique personal and literary insights into her dearest friend."

"How nice for Lucia's other friends to know that Miss Leg was the 'dearest.' She was certainly the dearest in terms of the expense all that food and wine!"

"I cannot disagree with you, Benjy. And now to the real news. If you can believe it, our dear Mayor and Chief Magistrate plans to erect a blue plaque on the frontage of Mallards to record for posterity that 'the renowned literary figure Susan Leg stayed there whilst visiting Tilling.'"

"Will it say,'once', Elizabeth?"

"It doesn't say, Benjy dear, but I suspect not. And, as if that were not enough re-writing of history, Lucia is very pleased to announce that she has founded and will chair a new society, 'The Amici di Rudolf da Vinci' to promote the estimable body of work of Susan Leg and her lengthy connection with her beloved Tilling."

"More like promote our dear Mayor," commented Benjy, certain that this was exactly what his wife wished to hear and relieved that for the foreseeable future her penetrating eye and malevolent critical faculties were bound to be focussed not on him but on Lucia.

"Well if that doesn't take the prize," frothed Elizabeth, "Not only does that woman invade us, take over my beautiful home and try to usurp my rightful place at the head of affairs in Tilling , but she falsely claims to be an intime of one of the very few world famous best friends I have ever had. Everyone knows I knew Susan Leg long before Lucia. I gave her hospitality here at Grebe and introduced her to my circle in Tilling. And here am I completely overlooked and ignored, as though I never existed. I have never been so insulted - jamais, jamais, jamais!"

"To be fair, Liz ," commented Benjy, after a longer interval than he would soon come to realise was advisable, "You did give Susan the heave-ho. After running her for a while you had more than enough of her freeloading and egotism. Tell the truth, weren't you relieved to off-load the old harpy onto unsuspecting Lucia?"

"How silly of me to expect any loyalty, let-alone support, from you Benjamin, especially after your last drunken performance at Mallards. You know very well that I lent Lucia my personal signed copy of Susan's 'Kind Hearts and Coronets' and from the moment she read it - pot-boiler or not - she longed to be immortalised in one of Susan's novels."

"It was pretty clear what Lucia was up to," admitted Benjy, "And then there was also that business with the silver at the Town Hall."

"Absolutely, Benjy, as if it wasn't bad enough that Lucia lures away my best friend, she then humiliates me - her very own Mayoress - by refusing to allow me to display our beautiful civic plate to a distinguished visitor to the town. As Mayoress I wasn't even allowed to invite Susan to sign the official civic Visitor's Book. Snub after snub - it really is too bad of Lucia and so typical."

But it was some time ago, Elizabeth. Don't you think it's time to let bygones be bygones?"

"I was perfectly happy to let the matter rest" replied Elizabeth slowly and patiently, as though addressing an idiot child, "But nothing entitles a parvenu like Lucia to claim in the "Tilling Gazette" that she rather than I was Susan Leg's oldest and dearest friend in Tilling. I will not be relegated to the status of a forgotten old relic stranded out here on the marshes. If Lucia really wants to put up a blue plaque outside my 'Mallards' it should say ' 'Elizabeth Mapp-Flint, leading citizen and benefactress of the town, once resided here.' That would do very nicely."

"Yes, of course, my dear," stammered Benjy in a belated and doomed effort to coral a horse long since bolted, "Anyone with the slightest sense knows that you were by far Susan's oldest friend."

"'Closest' dear, 'closest '- 'oldest' can mean quite another thing."

"Yes, of course, Elizabeth ...closest....friend in Tilling and that Lucia was just a late-comer and social climber at that."

"Too little , too late, ma cherie," commented Elizabeth archly, "But thank you for at least trying."

"So, what are you going to do?" asked Benjy, well knowing that Elizabeth was capable of virtually anything required to divert the spotlight from Lucia back onto herself.

"Fight fire with fire obviously Benjy, but speed will be of the essence."

At the marketing hour in the High Street next morning there was only one topic of conversation.

Outside Twistevant's shop, a small but distinguished group assembled. It comprised Tilling's spiritual guardian, Padre Kenneth Bartlett and his wife Evie, Algernon and Susan Wyse, Quaint Irene Coles and Diva Plaistow.

"Well, did you all get two invitations?" asked Diva.

"I'm afraid so," replied Algernon Wyse with bows first towards Mallards and then vaguely in the direction of Grebe. In a sorrowful tone that intimated something distasteful and unmentionable had occurred, "Yesterday evening Cadman delivered the invitation from Mrs Pillson."

"And this morning, Major Benjy called with Elizabeth's," added Susan.

"Exactly the same as us, tha noos," confirmed the Padre.

"And me," said Irene.

"So we are all invited to the inaugural meetings of Lucia's "Amici di Rudolf da Vinci" and Elizabeth's "The Susan Leg Society" at the same time on the same day?" said Diva.

"And to hear Elizabeth's personal account of her 'long friendship with the late literary legend entitled 'Susan Leg: As I knew Her'" explained Susan.

"And dear Lucia's recollections of her 'many happy moments in the company of Tilling's celebrated literary lioness 'Susan Leg ~ as she really was - by an intime'" enthused Irene, "I know which one I'm going to. Old Mappy's invitation is already in my dustbin."

Ignoring Irene's longstanding partiality, Diva remarked, "I really think it places us all in an impossible position"

"You speak for yourselves! "interjected Irene. "My position is quite possible. I shall be going to Mallards to hear my angel deliver her address and be the first to cough up a contribution for the new blue plaque. I don't see what all the fuss is about. We must all go to dearest Lucia's meeting and ignore the dreadful Mapp. It's obvious."

"I mean, what on earth are we supposed to do?" continued Diva, completely ignoring Irene's outburst,""If we accept one's invitation, we will mortify the other. Neither will ever forgive us."

"And social life in Tilling as we know it will be dead," added Algernon.

"Yet, again!" vSusan concurred.

"So what on earth shall we do, Mr Wyse?" implored Diva.

"If you will forgive my presumption ladies and gentlemen, I think that the solution is self-evident," continued Algernon soothingly, "If I might take the liberty of suggesting that you each consult your diaries, I think you will find that you are already engaged tomorrow evening. Pray correct me if I am mistaken, but some weeks ago did you all do Susan and myself the inestimable honour of accepting our invitation to join us for bridge and light refreshments at Starling Cottage tomorrow evening? I know we were particularly happy that we were able to secure your company at our humble residence at such a busy time of year. Naturally Susan and I regret that given these longstanding arrangements none of us will be disengaged and free to attend the inaugural meeting of either worthy literary society."

"Aye, of course, Mr Wyse ,"Thank ye for jogging my memory," replied the Padre, "So a decision between the two guid ladies disnae arise."

"And no-one's feelings need be hurt," squeaked Evie.

"Well, you can all do what you want," sniffed Irene, "I don't give a fig for your inventing' previous commitments. I, for one, will be heading for 'Mallards tomorrow night to hear my lovely Lucia's talk. Hopefully she may also play the piano. Beautifully, as always. I'm off!"

"Only to be expected," commented Diva, "Irene is so highly strung. Anyway thank you for reminding us about our prior engagement Mr Wyse. I must go home and write my replies. Au reservoir!"

"We must also repair to yon Vicarage and reply to both invitations. Good day, Mr and Mrs Wyse. Come Evie."

Once the consensus brokered by the sagacious Algernon Wyse had emerged, the entire Gathering - save for Quaint Irene - dispersed to implement it.

The next evening, Lucia showed Quaint Irene out of the front door of Mallards and waved to her as she headed forlornly towards the Traders Arms.

Entering the Garden Room, she turned to Georgie and sighed.

"Oh well," said Georgie gently, "I suppose it was only to be expected. We can always rely on Irene, but the others have to be more careful. Elizabeth was bound to resent your founding The Amici de Rudolf da Vinci. She thought you were stealing her limelight. And our friends do not wish to be seen to be taking sides."

"Even when I haven't done anything wrong?"said Lucia, sulkily

"You knew exactly what you were doing, Lucia."

"I suppose you're right" replied Lucia with surprising acquiescence, "But it's not as though I'm Herr Hitler. I didn't just march in and annex the Sudetenland. I suppose I had better telephone the stonemasons and cancel the blue plaque I commissioned to record dear Susan's many happy visits to Mallards.

"I think that would be best," confirmed Georgie,."Now will you treat me to a little po di musica whilst I dust my bibelots before we retire?"

"My Moonlight, Georgie?

"Divino, Lucia"

As Georgie applied his damp chamois to his Faberge cigarette case, Lucia languorously played the opening bars of the Slow Movement of the Moonlight Sonata with her silhouette caught by lamplight in the window of the Garden Room.

As Beethoven's mellifluous chords floated above the red roofs and thence over the marshes below the ancient walls of Tillling, a

solitary light burned in the drawing room window of Grebe.

"Yet another evening ruined by that ghastly woman, Benjy," said Elizabeth, poking the last vestiges of coal in the grate viciously with a large poker ,"All I wanted to do was to give my dear friends in Tilling some insight into my long and intense friendship with a person who happened to be a world famous literary figure. And they are all so frightened of upsetting Her Worship that every one of them turned down my invitation. Well, they can't say that I haven't done my very best to free them from the yoke of her tyranny."

"There, there Liz old girl," replied Benjy with an affectionate tone amplified by the three whiskey and sodas he had been able to consume after dinner whilst his life partner's vigilance was uncharacteristically diminished by her angst and irritation at her utter failure to convene the inaugural meeting of the Susan Leg Society.

"Don't upset yourself my sweet. Shall we make the most of it and get an early night - if you get my drift?"

"Oh, Benjy!...."

CHAPTER SEVEN: MALLARDS REVISITED

Summer in Tilling was differentiated from other seasons by the sport taking place.

As they had done since childhood, brothers Georgie and Per were the heart of their community and were at the helm of most sporting affairs.

Winter meant football at Tilling United FC with teams representing every age group from the under-sevens to veterans.

In the summer, it often seemed half the males in the town donned their whites and turned out to play cricket for Tilling.

Numerous asterisks on the sporting calendar flagged up important league games and ultra-competitive local derbies with neighbouring towns and villages including Brinton and Winchelsea.

As well as visits to and from other clubs in the county, the annual weekend visit to Tilling for the match against its Cricket Club was a popular fixture in the touring itinerary of several well-known ad hoc teams.

Each year, the height of summer was marked by the renewal of hotly contested competition between the pride of Sussex and sundry groups of visiting cricketers from a surprising range of backgrounds and professions.

Thus Tilling's teachers, lawyers, estate agents and council workers were pitted against similarly diverse bands of actors doctors, journalists and plumbers.

Exotic names of inveterate tourers included Wanderers, Zingari, Tulse Hill Casuals, Bromley Wanderers, Home and Colonial and Stoneyhurst Old Boys, each marked by a varied range of garish club blazers and badged and tasselled caps.

In the weeks following Inspector Morrison's departure, the dramatic schism over Irene Cole's portrait that tore the towns' elite asunder began to heal and social and civic life returned to,what for Tilling approached normal.

Mortified at the unpleasant consequences of the bullying and irresponsibility of a minority of over-boisterous members when drunk, Tilling Wheelers did their utmost to make amends.

The culprits were initially banished from the club for life until the merciful intervention of Lucia following her emergence from her coma.

Recognising that their actions stemmed more from youthful boisterousness than malice, Lucia as Patron and Life President of the Tilling Wheelers suggested that the wrongdoers be reinstated for a probationary period of two years and be encouraged to demonstrate their contrition and rehabilitation by undertaking some voluntary work in the community.

As well as leading cycling proficiency classes for local schoolchildren, the group of five Wheelers raised sufficient funds to buy for the young chorister so aggressively bounced by them a new bicycle plus an invitation to join them for the regular group rides in the area.

Now fully recovered from his ordeal by bouncing, the youth accepted the apologies and enjoyed his new bicycle.

This gesture also pacified his irate father who agreed not to press criminal charges or to proceed with the civil lawsuit being prepared by his solicitors.

As well as encouraging the Tilling Wheelers to make amends, Lucia also lost no time upon returning from her recuperatory villegiatura on the Continent in undoing the final act of wanton self aggrandisement undertaken by the Mayoress during the Mayor's indisposition.

Lucia shared the chagrin of many fellow citizens at a proposal forced through Tilling Council whilst the Mayor was hors de combat.

Elizabeth Mapp-Flint had, with the help of her own vote and those of Councillor Twistevant's cabal on the Council, managed to secure agreement to the change of name of the Belvedere Gardens beloved of generations of citizens as a place of quiet contemplation and respectful recollection of the glorious fallen war dead of the town.

Friends and neighbours were aghast to learn that she proposed to name the tranquil enclave as "The Caroline Mapp Memorial Garden."

"I simply cannot understand whatever possessed her," remarked Diva Plaistow, "It's not as though Elizabeth's auntie actually ever did anything for anyone. "

"Especially the people of Tilling; from what I've heard," added Irene Coles, "She didn't really like anyone,"

"Even her niece," agreed Diva, "It's just Elizabeth's way of using her aunt to make her mark."

"And getting one over on my dear angel, Lucia," concluded Irene, "She ought to know better. It was inevitable that Lucia would prevail, right always comes out on top! So ya boo sucks to Old Mappy; failed again."

The Bank Holiday weekend saw a tumult of activity around the town which was thronged to the eaves with visitors eager to view and photograph the civic ceremonial and watch some cricket.

On Friday the entire corporation processed from the Town Hall around the narrow cobbled streets to the Norman Church of St Marys where the Padre was to conduct the annual service of thanks for the work of the officers and officials of the council.

As he had in the ceremonial before the ill-fated revival of Beating the Bounds, the Town Clerk preceded the Mayor and other councillors wearing their robes, dashing feathered hats and the insignia of office.

In his dress uniform, including snowy white silk stockings

and silver buckled patent leather pumps, the Clerk carried the priceless jewelled silver mace of the town.

On returning to the Town Hall from St Mary's Church, the mace was placed on public display with the other civic plate of Tilling for the remainder of the busy day.

On Saturday morning, the first eleven of Tilling Cricket Club began its fixture with the visiting Home and Colonial Club on its annual tour of Kent and Sussex.

The Home and Colonial was an occasional team with no fixed ground of its own, which gathered together at intervals to tour and play against other amateur clubs in the south east and Home Counties.

It's members were largely drawn from expatriate foreign office, tea and coffee planters or commercial men who had spent most of their careers in India, Aftrica and the Far East from the days of Empire.

They returned to Blighty at fixed intervals on leave or eventually in retirement all bearing weathered tans and some with impressive cricketing skills.

The sports bags and luggage unloaded from the touring charabanc of the team bore numerous faded and torn stickers.

The distressed labels told of countless passages on P&O to take up posts in offices with rotating ceiling fans in sweltering cities of the Empire or remote plantations up country.

Cricket filled many hours on otherwise empty evenings and endless Sunday afternoons far from home. If adultery and alcoholism were excluded, there was often precious little else to do.

This practice in perfecting batting and bowling technique frequently yielded dividends many   years later in soundly defeating their stay-at-home opponents.

This annual event was as much a social occasion as a sporting one.

As Mayor and President of the Club, Lucia presided over the initial formalities and was introduced to both teams prior to tossing the coin to determine who batted first.

The Mayor and Georgie Pillson then took seats on the verandah outside the pavilion with the Mayoress, Major Benjy and other Councillors and prominent citizens.

Spectators at the cricket match also included Herbert and Bunty Morrison who had returned for the first time to visit family, six months after moving to London.

That morning Herbert enjoyed a reunion with boyhood best friends, Georgie and Per.

Herbert had spent his childhood with the twins living next door in one of Harold Twistevant's "picturesque cottages" near to the station.

On arriving back in Tilling, he and Bunty had been fascinated to see that their childhood stamping ground was being demolished.

A council sign nearby proudly proclaimed that, "On completion of the Tilling Railway Cuttings Slum Clearance Scheme #1 Desirable Modern Residences will be constructed on the site under the name 'Twistevant Mansions.'"

The implausibility of this renaming amused Harold and Bunty no-end and prompted a new private game over the weekend involving the invention of improbable institutions.

Early suggestions included "The Count Dracula Blood Bank " and "Attila the Hun Pacifists Union."

As the weekend proceeded, suggestions became more indiscreet and topical and included, "The Benjamin Flint Teatotallers Society" and "The Irene Coles School of Tact and Diplomacy."

◆ ◆ ◆

The visitors won the toss and opted to bat first.

The spectators sitting in front of the pavilion applauded enthusiastically as Tilling's eleven took the field.

As they did so, Herbert turned to Bunty and commented how nostalgic it made him feel, "I did this with Georgie and Per for twenty years," he remarked, "We had the best times playing for Tilling,"

"I know Herbert," she replied, "You should have brought your whites."

"I'm not sure I'm good enough for the first eleven nowadays," he joked, "Perhaps the third team on a quiet day!"

The Morrisons broke off from their banter to join in the applause as the visitor's openers left the pavilion and strode out towards the wicket.

The batsmen's tans demonstrated the effect of years beneath the colonial sun that gave their club its name.

Both sported greying beards that gave a startling resemblance to the late, great W.G.Grace of England and Gloucestershire, who they were about to seek to emulate.

◆ ◆ ◆

Spectators enjoyed an entertaining morning's play beneath a clear sky with gulls wheeling and shrieking on a refreshing onshore breeze.

Home and Colonial soon amassed two hundred and twenty runs for six wickets and their opener was still not out and approaching a century.

Over lunch, whilst Bunty chatted to her sisters, Herbert shared a table with friends Georgie and Per.

After catching up with news of the last six months, conversation turned to the morning's play and particularly the brilliant performance of the visitors' opening batsman.

"Jolly good knock that" enthused Georgie

"Played like a professional, "added Per, "A bit too good for us here in Tilling."

"You're right there, old chap," joked Herbert, "I've not seen cover drives like that since Wally Hammond at the Oval. I'm not sure how you're going to get him out."

"Better hope they declare soon, to give us a sporting chance!" chimed both twins, in unison, as was still so often the case.

"The thing is, I could swear I've seen him before - especially his strokes on the leg side. It's driving me mad, but I just can't remember," said Herbert

"You better have another pint to help your memory" quipped Per.

"Good idea, brother" added Georgie, "Get one for me too."

Although Lucia and Georgie Pillson had invited Herbert and Bunty to dine with them at Mallards that evening, the Morrisons were obliged to decline owing to a prior commitment.

They had a longstanding arrangement to spend the evening with close family and friends on what would be their first evening back home in Tilling since relocating to London.

A dinner and dance to celebrate the golden wedding anniversary of Bunty's parents had been arranged in the function room of the Kings Arms in the High Street

The Mayor completely understood that family must come first and happily replaced the invitation to dine with tea the following afternoon. The Morrisons were pleased to accept.

Later that night after a convivial family meal and touching speeches and toasts, the music and dancing had started.

Wallflowers for the time being, Herbert sat and chatted with Georgie and Per.

As it had done so many times over the years, their conversation turned to the day's play at Tilling Cricket Club against the formidable Home and Colonial.

"Enjoyable game, but we eventually lost by an innings and twenty runs," commented Per morosely.

"Largely due to that opening batsman of theirs" added Georgie.

"Yes, I saw his innings. Quite a player," sympathised Herbert,

"It's still driving me mad, but I'm sure I remember him from somewhere"

"I know what you mean - especially that amazing cover drive," replied Georgie. But just as he was about to continue, his young cousin Norman, a constable with the Tilling Police, walked in.

"I'm glad you could make it, Norman," said Per, who had invited him to pop in if he had time after coming off duty, "Help yourself to a drink, now you've finished your shift. You know Herbert, of course"

"Absolutely Per," he replied, extending his hand "Nice to see you again, Inspector."

"It's Assistant Commissioner now," added Georgie, "He's gone up in the world since leaving our poor little Tilling."

"No, we're off duty; 'Herbert' will be fine, Norman," laughed Herbert, adding, "But you can still call me 'Sir,' Per".

"Thanks, Herbert. I would like to stay for a drink, but I have to go back to the station in a minute. All hell has broken out at the Town Hall tonight"

"What's going on?" asked all three in unison.

"I'm surprised you haven't heard already. There's uproar in the town. The Civic Plate was on display for the holiday crowds and the Mace has gone missing. Disappeared into thin air. The Mayor and Town Clerk are absolutely furious."

"No!" came the response in triplicate, this being the time-honoured observation invariably made in Tilling on the receipt of particularly shocking news."

"You had better get back to the station to lend a hand," suggested Herbert, "Duty comes first. Please tell Inspector Newman that I am here over the weekend and would be happy to help however I can. I'm anxious not to interfere though."

"Yes, Sir," said the young officer as he turned to leave the function room and return to the police station."

As the evening progressed, news filtered though to the Kings Arms from the Town Hall and police station.

It emerged that, within the hour, a brief anonymous phone call has been received by the Town Clerk urging "If you want to find the Mace again try looking for it out at Grebe."

With the help of the GPO, it had been possible to trace the call to a public phone box in nearby Brinton, but by the time the police had arrived there, the caller had long since gone.

With some trepidation, Herbert Morrison's successor as Senior Officer, Inspector Newman, explained to the Mayoress and her increasingly irritable spouse that anonymous tip-off had been received and that they would have no alternative but to search and rule out the possibility.

"The very idea is preposterous, young, boomed Major Benjy aggressively.

"This is simple slander. Such a vile outrage would never have taken place in the time of good Inspector Morrison," wailed Elizabeth, "But you had better come in and do your worse. You must not however, be surprised if this squalid intrusion results in civil proceedings against both your force and you personally."

Within minutes of commencing the search, a sergeant called Inspector Newman to a shed in the garden at the rear of the property.

There, wrapped in a dusty tiger skin rug, concealed beneath a pile of dented assagais and two sweat-stained solar topees, lay the silver jewelled mace bearing the crest of the ancient Borough of Tilling.

"No, it can't possibly be," screamed Eliabeth Mapp-Flint on learning of the discovery, "It has nothing to do with us. It must have been planted. I am the Mayoress of Tilling. My husband is a distinguished retired army officer. Do we look like common thieves? And what on earth would we do with a mace of all things? It's hardly easy to conceal is it? I could hardly take it with me in my shopping baket in the High Street each morning."

"Precisely, Mrs Mapp-Flint. Perhaps that's why we discovered it on your property so quickly," said Inspector Newman, "I'm afraid that it will be necessary to go to the station to look into the matter further. Please both come with me in the police car and we will go back to Tilling to sort the matter out."

"Look here young man. You heard what my wife said; she's the Mayoress and I'm an officer and gentleman. You can't arrest us just like that."

"Your wife is the Mayoress and you are an officer and gentleman who both happen to have a priceless stolen jewelled mace in the shed next to your lawn mower, Major. I'm afraid I have no alternative but to ask you come with me to to answer some questions. Now, may we go?"

The Mapp-Flints exchanged a silent glance and nodded.

Without a further word they sat down in the back of the police car and were driven towards Tilling.

As news of the recovery of the mace from its surprising hiding place reached the Kings Arms, Herbert Morrison jumped to his feet, muttering "I've got it; I knew it would come to me eventually!

If you will excuse me, I need to make an important telephone call."

From the public telephone outside the salon bar in the Kings Arms Herbert soon dialled the familiar number of Tilling Police Station and asked to be put through to the duty senior officer.

CHAPTER EIGHT: EPILOGUE

Sunday mornings in Tilling were generally quite a tranquil contrast to the frenetic evening before and this was no exception.

At Glebe, tense silence prevailed.

Elizabeth and Benjamin Map -Flint sat at the breakfast table silent and shocked.

Both stared ahead expressionless and seemingly wholly vacant.

Fried eggs, bacon and a solitary halved tomato, crowned with a limp sprig of parsley sat uneaten on each white plate before them, slowly congealing.

The Sunday newspapers remained pristine, unopened and unread on the sideboard nearby.

The previous day Tilling, police to whom Mrs Mapp-Flint would often complain over their inept failure to bring to justice the recidivist scrumping of her precious Cox's Orange Pippins, had searched Grebe unbidden and unannounced, discovered stolen property secreted there, arrested the couple and publicly taken them into custody for several hours of blunt interrogation.

The pair had been bailed from the police station and not yet extended the courtesy of any further explanation whatsoever.

The only thought of which Elizabeth Mapp-Flint could muster that morning was,"Could my life be any worse?"

Given that any expressed thought or opinion was certain to invoke the most vicious response from his spouse, Major Benjy prudently maintained a mind so blank as to be entirely devoid of thought.

In Tilling , the telephone at Mallards rang repeatedly as friends clamoured for news of what had happened to the civic mace and whether the culprit had yet been found.

Lucia Pillson did not feel it appropriate to disseminate such information as was yet available regarding this shocking event other than to confirm that the mace and entirety of the civic plate were perfectly safe and sound within the vaults beneath the Town Hall.

She did not wish to trouble Inspector Newman unnecessarily on Sunday and felt confident that a full briefing would be forthcoming at the earliest possible moment

Accordingly, the Mayor and Georgie Pillson attended Sunday service in Tilling church and did not gather with friends before and after the service to exchange news or participate in the gossip and conjecture predictably resulting form the absence of the Mapp- Flints from their usual pew in church.

Nervousness about the outcome of investigation into the dramatic theft meant the Pillson's did not trouble cook to prepare Sunday lunch and planned instead to take tea with the Morrisons when they called at Mallards that afternoon.

Having left the twins to enjoy the last afternoon of their visit with their grandparents, Herbert and Bunty stood outside the shiny black front door of Mallards at three.

As Foljambe showed the visitors into the Garden Room, Georgie stood up to welcome them and bade them take a seat.

They could see that Lucia was engaged on the telephone and gathered from a gesture and mouthed words of apology that she was sorry and would be with them shortly.

The Morrisons nodded understandingly and awaited their hostess.

Shortly Lucia put down the black Bakelite receiver and rose to greet her guests with profuse apologies and a welcoming handshake, "I do apologise, but I simply had to take that phone call from Inspector Newman. I do hope you don't think me rude?"

"Of course not Your Worship,"replied Herbert, slipping back into his mode of address of previous years.

"Now, now, Herbert," admonished Lucia, "I thought we had banished that - a relict of a bygone age - 'Lucia' please"

"Of course..Lucia," said Herbert, apologetically, " I think we may have some news to exchange about yesterday's events,"

"Indeed we do," replied Lucia, " Inspector Newman said you had been most helpful in clarifying the Mace Case."

"Oh Lucia, you rhymed," joked Georgie, trying to lighten the atmosphere, "Shall I call for tea?"

Lucia agreed that this would be a good idea and as Georgie did her bidding, she reported further on her briefing from Herbert's successor, "So Inspector Newman informed me that the mace was found safe and sound in a shed at Grebe, but that other than this fact there is no evidence that the 'householders' had anything to do with the theft."

"So the Mapp-Flints are in the clear?" asked Georgie.

"Yes, dear, so it appears from the information now to hand. We really must inform them of this at some point after the weekend."

"They must be worried," he observed, "Very worried."

"Indeed, Georgie, indeed," she replied, "But all due inquiries must be completed first. This brings me to your contribution to resolving the mystery, Herbert, and your telephone call last night. Are you free to tell us what happened?

"I think so," said Herbert, modestly adding, " I don't want to overstate my part in solving the case. It suddenly dawned on me how and why I knew the opening batsman of the Home and Colonial"

"And how was that?" asked Georgie, spellbound.

"Under that long hair, bushy beard and deep tan was someone very well known to us in Tilling and with strong links to Tilling and indeed Mallards itself."

""And?" Asked Georgie now beside himself with curiosity

"I realised that it was young Henry Mapp, who often opened the batting for Tilling when Georgie, Per and I used to play. I knew I recognised that brilliant cover drive of his anywhere. Naturally I reported that to Inpector Newman and when he was brought to the station, Henry admitted that he had taken the mace. "

"But what was he doing here again and why should he do that?" asked Georgie.

"That's quite a complicated question, Georgie, remarked Lucia."Let us enjoy our tea and then try to get to the bottom of it. The other thing I wanted to mention stemmed from my conversation a few minutes ago with Inspector Newman"

"Oh, yes, what was that,"asked Herbert, intrigued

"Inspector Newman said that the questioning of Mr Mapp had advanced as far as it usefully could today and that it had to be determined whether to charge him and remand him in custody or perhaps simply release on police bail pending further inquiries."

"Like the Mapp-Flints?" asked Georgie

"Indeed Mr Georgie," replied Herbert, "And what does Inspector Newman actually propose to do?"

"That is where the position seems a little unusual," Lucia replied, "It seems Mr Mapp has specifically asked to be allowed to visit Mallards and to speak to me and his old friend Herbert Morrison."

"How exciting!" exclaimed Georgie, "And can we allow that Herbert?"

" I don't see why not," replied Herbert, " I think I can safely say that the case of the missing mace involves many other complicated issues and that no single one can be completely resolved without understanding the others. To stand any chance of clearing the matter up, we need to hear what Henry has to say and to ask him some questions"

"I agree entirely, Herbert, " replied Lucia, "If you - and indeed poor Bunty - can spare the time to help us resolve this mystery , I know Tilling would, as ever, be most grateful"

"Of course, Lucia," Herbert replied, "Bunty and I would like nothing more than help to clear this up, so please go ahead." "Absolutely," added Bunty, who if truth be known, like Georgie Pillson, was a fascinated onlooker.

Some ten minutes later, Grosvenor entered the Garden Room and informed Lucia, "A Mr Henry Mapp is at the door, Ma'am accompanied by a police constable."

"Very well, Grosvenor," she replied, "Please show Mr Mapp in and perhaps you could take the constable to the staff hall and offer him some refreshments?"

Shortly afterwards a tanned and bearded middle age man entered the Garden Room, dressed in the gaudy striped blazer of the Home & Colonial, white flannels and cricket boots.

"Good afternoon, Mrs Pillson," he said, extending his hand.

"How do you do?" she replied, "May I introduce my husband Georgie? I think you already know Assistant Commissioner, Sir Herbert Morrison and his wife, Lady Bunty?"

"Indeed, I do, Mrs Pillson, we go, back a long way, even before he was a lowly constable, let alone a knight of the realm!"

As introductions and reunions were completed, further tea was served and the hosts and visitors took their seats.

"Thank you for agreeing to see me in your home, Your Worship," Henry Mapp began, "Little did I think I should ever cross the threshold of dear old Mallards again, let alone direct from a police cell."

"I can quite understand how you feel Mr Mapp," responded the Mayor, "Inspector Newman said that you were anxious to explain yourself and we certainly have some questions to ask after yesterday's dramatic events. Perhaps I might begin by asking what actually happened yesterday and what on earth you were thinking of?"

"Of course, Mrs Pillson, I will do my best. I didn't come back to Tilling with a specific plan in mind but yesterday was overwhelming for me."

"I can well imagine that Mr Mapp. What exactly overwhelmed you?"

"Well, as you might expect after all those years away, it felt strange to walk down those steps from the pavilion again and open the batting in Tilling - even though it was for the opposition"

"You had a splendid knock," added Herbert, "A match-winning innings like you used to have when opening with Georgie or Per all those years ago."

"Very true, old friend," Henry replied, "I was seeing the ball very clearly that morning. It was like being in heaven: 'Et in Arcadia ego' sort of thing, like we learned in classics back at school. The trouble was, when I walked up back to the pavilion I saw her sitting there with that great lump of lard of a husband of hers. There she was holding court in her Mayoress chain of office, spouting nonsense about this that and the other to anyone daft enough to listen whilst he sneaked off for a pink gin from the bar whilst she was preoccupied blowing her own trumpet."

His listeners knew exactly what Henry Mapp meant. Everyone in the room had at some time or other been infuriated by the pretensions of the Mapp-Flints, though no-one was outspoken enough to say so in the Garden Room that day.

"Anyway, it was as though something in my mind exploded," he explained, "I just decided on the spur of the moment and did it."

"And how exactly did you go about it, Henry?" asked Herbert gently.

"Nothing particularly cunning actually," he replied, " I used the time after I was eventually out. I was still wearing my whites with my blazer and carried my cricket bag. You would be surprised how little attention a chap in whites carrying a cricket bag around the town on a summer Saturday attracts."

"So you simply walked to the Town Hall?"

"Yes, Mayor; it only took a couple of minutes. I just joined the queue to see the civic plate on display. In the line I racked my brain about what to do. Then I remembered the times when we were children and the Mayor would throw hot pennies down from the balcony of the Kings Arms."

"We only warm them ever so slightly now, remarked Georgie Pillson, pleased at last to make some contribution to proceedings, "Too many injuries, you know; we kept getting sued. It's all Health and Safety, nowadays, isn't it?"

"Thank you, Georgie dear," interrupted the Mayor, "I'm sure Mr Mapp doesn't need to hear about our quaint local customs and more litigious citizens. Now Mr Mapp, you were saying? What did you do next?"

"Well, Mayor, I took a handful of loose change out of my pocket and threw it in the air. As you might imagine, mayhem ensued as most of the queue and the staff on duty scrabbled around on the floor for the coins."

"How ingenious!" commented Georgie

"And then, whilst everyone was distracted, I just lifted the mace from its stand and slipped it into my cricket bag. It fitted perfectly, just like a bat. And then I just slipped away and nobody seemed to notice."

"And then what did you do?' asked Herbert.

"The timing was perfect. I got on the tram which goes out to the golf course. At that time of day, it was empty and I jumped off as it passed Grebe."

"And you weren't seen out there either, by the servants or any walkers or trippers?"

"Not so far as I know, Herbert. I used the big hornbeam hedge as cover from the house and the road. It was easy to slip into the garden shed to hide the mace. I just wrapped it up in a moth-eaten tiger-skin rug and covered it in some dusty old rubbish."

"That's how we all think of Major Benjy's precious souvenirs of the Raj," commented Georgie.

"So, then I jumped on the next tram and made my way back in time for the afternoon's play. The team then caught the charabanc to Brinton to stay overnight before our next fixture."

"And when you arrived, you telephoned the Town Clerk with a tip-off about where the mace was hidden?" asked Lucia.

"Yes, I did," admitted Henry, "And then I just waited for news - until the police turned up and took me back to Tilling."

"That was possible after you remembered where you had seen Mr Mapp before and telephoned Inspector Newman, wasn't it, Herbert?" asked Lucia.

"Indeed, Mayor," confirmed Herbert, "But tell us, Henry, you explained so clearly how you removed and hid the mace but what we really need to know now is exactly why you did it."

"That's really why I wanted so much to talk to you all today,"admitted Henry, "I think you all know it all stems from my cousin Elizabeth, and I imagine some of you may already have suspicions about what I'm now going to say."

"I think you may well be right" confirmed Herbert, who in reality was virtually certain about what his childhood friend was going to divulge. It had been rumoured in Tilling for many years.

"Please carry on, Mr Mapp, added Lucia, We will try not to interrupt."

"Thank you both. I'll start at the beginning and try to keep it simple," Henry began, "As you both know, I spent a lot of happy days as a child here in Tilling."

"You fitted in really well here, old chap. You had heaps of friends and we had great time playing cricket and out and about on our bikes with the Wheelers. And your Aunt Caroline thought the world of you"

"Absolutely, Herbert, that's where the trouble began. I had the best of times with you and the others and I was Aunt Caroline's favourite. To be honest, I never thought she really liked cousin Elizabeth. She was always too pushy and just tried too hard. Auntie always saw straight through her."

"Again, we know exactly what you mean," commented Lucia.

"She really hasn't changed much at all" added Georgie.

"Elizabeth could never come to terms with the fact that Aunt Caroline preferred me to her. She and her mother always planned that Elizabeth should inherit Mallards"

"And you stood in her way?" asked Lucia.

"And so when the so-called priceless stolen Mapp Diadem was found not very well hidden in my bedroom, I was wrongfully blamed. I knew it was Elizabeth who had planted it to ensure that I got the blame."

"And guaranteed that she got Mallards? " interrupted Georgie.

"I believed that the criminal term is 'fitted up' isn't it, Herbert?"

asked Lucia.

"Yes, it is. There was never enough evidence to prosecute anyone for the theft and understandably Caroline Mapp was unwilling to press charges against her once-beloved nephew."

"So, my punishment was that I was sent away by Aunt Caroline and never invited to Mallards again."

"Until today," suggested Georgie with an unnerving sense of the obvious.

"Obviously, I was cut out of the will entirely and when Aunt Caroline died, Mallards and her entire estate passed to Cousin Elizabeth."

"And what happened to you then?" asked Lucia.

"To say I was 'under a cloud' is a massive understatement. Although I was not charged with theft of the diadem, my family and all the world treated me as if I were guilty."

"And?"

"Instead going to Cambridge and then to Sandhurst and my father's regiment as had been planned, I was bundled off to be a planter up country in Kenya. I was the proverbial black sheep, out of sight, out of mind and only allowed back on leave every two years."

"It seems so unfair," sympathised Bunty who until now had maintained a strict silence during what seemed to be semi-official business, but whose heart went out to her childhood friend.

"I made the best of it," responded Henry "I enjoyed the travel and played a lot of cricket, but I always felt my life was knocked off course by that woman."

"Just because of her jealousy and ruthlessness in getting what she wanted," he continued, "Everything was completely turned upside down. And what's worse; there was nothing at all that I could do about it. I was completely powerless. She had everything and I had nothing."

A tear ran down his tanned cheek as he continued, "On the day of the cricket match, all those years of pain caught up with me and just boiled over. I took the mace and put it where I did, not for money or personal gain. Just for once I wanted Cousin Elizabeth to feel some little part of the agony and humiliation I suffered because of her cruelty and greed. I wanted her to understand and perhaps to feel sorry for what she had done to me."

"Many of us who have remained here in Tilling with Elizabeth understand how you feel much better than you know, Mr Mapp," sympathised Lucia.

"I agree entirely with Mrs Pillson," added Herbert, "None of your many friends here had any doubt about your honesty and integrity. We wanted to tell you that but they shipped you off so quickly after the scandal that we were never given the chance."

"Just as Elizabeth Mapp and her mother wanted," added Bunty who, like her husband, had witnessed these events at the time. "For true Tillingites you were always that nice boy who joined in with us whenever he was here and never put a foot wrong. So Henry, you were never a black sheep here."

"I should also add that we have never really had any illusions about Elizabeth Mapp and her ways - neither then nor now," explained Lucia." But Tilling had always been remarkably tolerant of its inhabitants, even those who's conduct verges upon the unforgivable,"

As her listeners nodded in agreement, Lucia added"Although in this case perhaps the leniency went far too far, to your personal cost. All I can say is that we are all really sorry that Elizabeth succeeded in her underhand plan and took for herself what was rightfully yours."

"Thank you Mrs Pillson, that means great deal to me," Henry

replied, "I would love to think that one day I might retire here to Tilling without being suspected of being a common thief. I can't however deny that I did remove and hide the mace - even though I was never going to keep it. So I suppose I will always have to live with that."

Moved by his old friends comments, Herbert broke his recent silence, "If the Mayor and indeed 'her' Inspector Newman will allow me to intrude and comment upon current police affairs in Tilling?"

"Pray continue Herbert," replied Lucia - employing her benign magisterial nod, usually reserved for the Bench of Tilling Magistrates.

"Thank you Lucia. I think it is clear from the established facts of this case that there was no evidence of any express intention on the part of Mr Mapp to deprive the Council permanently of possession of the mace which had been recovered intact and undamaged. He is demonstrably not guilty of the offence of theft."

"Agreed," responded Lucia.

"Nor do I think, in all the circumstances, particularly bearing in mind the palpable historic injustice to Mr Mapp," suggested Herbert, "That the police will think it in the public interest to pursue a charge against him for any attempt to pervert the course of justice or even for wasting police time,"

" I concur completely, " said Lucia.

"Also, being realistic, I think it is wholly unlikely that the Mapp-Flints, as owners of Grebe, will wish to press charges for the unauthorised entry into their garden shed."

"Also agreed," she added, " Despite being upset at the discovery of the made upon her property, I hardly think Elizabeth would wish to risk discussion in open court of the possible actual guilty party in the temporary loss of the Mapp diadem all those years ago. I will ask Inspector Newman to explain this fully to my Mayoress and her husband when at some time next week he finds time to call upon them to confirm that it is unlikely that they will be facing criminal charges arising from the misplacing of the civic mace. "

"Thank you Mayor and Herbert, that it very fair-minded of you," responded Henry, adding "And in the meantime, I suppose they can sweat?"

Neither Lucia nor Herbert commented upon this latter suggestion, but merely smiled.

Lucia continued, "If Herbert would not mind me imposing more official duty into his leisure time, I think we should now make a telephone call to Inspector Newman to review the case of the mace and our discussions today. We might also discharge his constable, who I believe is still drinking tea and eating cake in our servant's hall and most importantly arrange for Mr Mapp to be released to rejoin his cricket tour?"

"A very pleasant duty, Lucia," agreed Herbert, "I'm afraid Henry will be too late for the match against Brinton today. I'm sure his batting will have been missed."

Relieved to hear he would now be freed, Henry remarked, "In some ways it feels as though history has at long last gone full circle. My anxiety over the missing diadem is now mirrored by my cousin's feeling of jeopardy over the missing mace."

"The difference being of course that your distress has persisted for thirty years and her's for only a matter days," noted Lucia drily.

"That is quite true," observed Henry, "But in recent years I have learned how Elizabeth managed to lose her precious Mallards as a result of her own foolishness and mismanagement - even though she blamed everyone else, including and perhaps especially you,

Your Worship, for her reversal of fortune,"

"She certainly has," responded Lucia with feeling.

"From what I know of her - and very sadly for me, that is a great deal - the loss of Mallards and knowledge that you now reside happily there, has been the very greatest reverse that cousin Elizabeth could contemplate. Living in exile on the marsh out at Grebe, looking every day towards Mallards at the very heart of Tilling, must surely be purgatory for her, if not absolute hell. In some ways, her exile so close to home must be more painful than mine on a tea plantation thousands of miles away."

"How very perceptive and wise, Henry," replied Herbert, "And please rest assured that, unlike your cousin, you have many genuine friends here in Tilling, who respect your true character and will always welcome you back."

Henry Mapp simply smiled and shook the hand of his oldest friend from childhood.

As he turned to leave the Garden Room, he doffed his Home and Colonial cap and was gone.

Within the hour, Herbert and Bunty Morrison had bidden farewell to Lucia and Georgie Pillson on the steps of Mallards with promises (unlikely to be kept) "to be sure to dine when next in town or Tilling."

Their twins, James and Dorothy were soon collected from grandparents and following more meaningful adieus, embraces and much waving, the black Metropolitan Police Riley drove through the Landgate and headed north towards London.

◆ ◆ ◆

At the same time, a constable from Tilling Police drove Henry Mapp, still wearing his brightly striped blazer and cricket whites, to Brinton to rejoin his team on tour.

Within a week he had boarded the P&O liner, RMS Orcadia bound for Mombassa and the long dusty treck back up to his remote plantation in the hills.

The drama of the missing mace and his return to Mallards had been cathartic. As he disembarked again beneath the burning East African sun, Henry Mapp no longer felt that he was returning to shameful exile. In revisiting Mallards, he had found redemption.

Meanwhile in the dining room at Grebe , Elizabeth and Major Benjamin Mapp-Flint sat at either end of the polished mahogany table, like so much else in the room inherited from dear Aunt Caroline. By force of habit, the pair had dressed for dinner.

Bowls of cook's undistinguished Brown Windsor soup sat before them cooling and uneaten.

Neither spoke and the only sound was the unsettling tick of the marble clock on the mantle.

The room was angst-ridden and the air preoccupied with listening for the heavy crunch of police boots upon the cinder path leading to the front door.

Each passing moment without news from the police station in Tilling added to their unspoken agony.

And they waited.

When tea things had been cleared and the Garden Room returned to order by the combined efforts of the ever-efficient Foljambe and Grosvenor, Lucia and Georgie Pillson sat down with a combined sigh of relief that usually preceded a thorough review of a significant day's events.

Georgie began what in some quarters might be considered "a debrief," "Your Herbert has lost none of his perspicacity, has he?"

"Indeed, not," she replied, "He still has that combination of acute intelligence and analytical skill combined with empathy and the common touch. Quite unique and so effective in his work. We shall not see his equal, although I am very pleased with our Inspector Newman."

"Coming on nicely," said Georgie, for once resisting the obvious pun, "He seems to have made an excellent start, don't you think?"

"Commendable." agreed Lucia, "I do not want to disturb him again on a Sunday evening, but will make a point of congratulating him on his handling of that unfortunate business over the mace when I speak to him tomorrow. "

"You really need to arrange for him to put Elizabeth and Benjy out of their misery about whether they will be charged for having the stolen property in their garden shed," suggested Georgie, "They must be in a terrible state waiting to hear."

"Absolutely dear, but I think that can wait until last least Wednesday, don't you? And thank you for not making a joke about the mace 'being planted in the potting shed'"

"My pleasure, Lucia. The delay should keep them quiet until then. I don't think we will be seeing them chatting outside Twstevants any time soon."

"And then, of course, we will have to decide whether to let Elizabeth know that we now know what really happened to the

Mapp diadem all those year ago."

"Of course, Lucia, and how Elizabeth actually came to inherit Mallards from dear aunt Caroline"

"When you come to think of it, now that Herbert and Bunty have returned to London and Henry is off to his plantation in Kenya, we are the only ones in Tilling - other than Elizabeth - who actually know her terrible guilty secret."

"And what are we going to do, Lucia?"

"Nothing for the moment, Georgie, absolutely nothing. This information is far too valuable to waste without any real need, despite how pleasurable it might be. We must keep it to ourselves until we really need to bring Elizabeth into line again. My Mayoress may be quiet for now, but people like her cannot suppress their real character indefinitely and we are bound to need to use it before long."

"Oh, Lucia, 'oo vewwy norty," said Georgie, "Time for ickle Mozartino?"

"Divino, Georgino mio!"

And they played.

THE END

ABOUT THE AUTHOR

Deryck J. Solomon

Birmingham-born Deryck is a retired Solicitor and Company Secretary. He spent his early childhood in Hampshire, Malta and Australia whilst his father served in the Royal Navy.

Returning to Birmingham in time to take the 11-plus, he attended the County High School in Redditch. After taking a degree in Modern History at Keble College, Oxford, he qualified as a lawyer and spent most of his career with a Midlands-based public company.

An aficionado of E.F.Benson's comic novels, he has compiled a light-hearted reference companion for readers, "A Mapp & Lucia Glossary."

He has published a trilogy of spin-off novels set in Benson's Tilling: "Inspector Morrison's Case Book,""Inspector Morrison: Another Year in Tilling"and "Inspector Morrison's Case Book Concluded."

"Mallards Revisited" is his first novel set in Tilling following the departure of Inspector Morrison to London.

He has also written a "An Innocent Abroad," a childhood memoir,

"Tales from Vaysey Pastures," a collection of profiles and horsey stories from an English livery yard and "Colonel Moseley: Still Waiting for the Great Leap Forward," a compendium of assorted reviews and articles .

He likes to paint, eat out and read and lives near Warwick with his partner, John, rescue dog Winnie and senior cob David.

Printed in Great Britain
by Amazon

24588915R00066